Aurat Durbar

Writings by Women
of South Asian Origin

AURAT

DURBAR

THE COURT OF WOMEN

WRITINGS BY WOMEN OF

SOUTH ASIAN ORIGIN

EDITED BY

FAUZIA RAFIQ

ACKNOWLEDGEMENTS

Contributors for their patience; Lasanda Kurukulasuriya and Smita Vir Tyagi for editorial support; Second Story women for a supportive, respectful and vibrant work environment; Mariam and Yermiah Khan Durrani for word processing; Rhea Tregebov for giving it a fine shape; Margie Wolfe for easing the process.

CANADIAN CATALOGUING IN PUBLICATION DATA

Aurat durbar : writings by women of South Asian origin

ISBN 0-929005-70-8

1. English literature – South Asian authors. 2. English literature – Women authors. 3. South Asians – Literary collections. 4. Women – Literary collections. I. Rafiq, Fauzia.

PN6069.W65A87 1995   820.8'09287   C95-931029-0

Copyright © 1995 by Fauzia Rafiq

Edited by Rhea Tregebov
Cover illustration
Detail from *Untitled* by Anoli Perera

Printed and bound in Canada

Second Story Press gratefully acknowledges the assistance of The Canada Council and the Ontario Arts Council

Published by
SECOND STORY PRESS
720 Bathurst Street, Suite 301
Toronto, Canada
M5S 2R4

We are bringing these flowers
In remembrance of all the women who had died
In all the wars that men have fought

We weep
We do not forget
And as we remember, we dedicate ourselves
To making a new world where we can all live free.

Graffiti seen off Cubbon Road,
Bangalore, India, May, 1990

Courtesy: Lasanda Kurukulasuriya

CONTENTS

PREFACE

Aurat Durbar.

Many women. Or one.

Affirms our diversity, self-empowerment, sexuality, the colour of our skin.

The voices that emerge in this anthology, individually and together, are forceful and unique. Diversity of content, language and expression challenge the reader like none other to an openness of the inner eye. *Aurat Durbar* is persistent, vocal, poetic, brave. Sharing visions, beauty, struggles, diversities, commonalities, passion, pleasure and pain.

Most languages of South Asia, both in our literary and folk tradition, favour poetry over prose as a form of story-telling and for the expression of profound feelings and passions. In this *mela* of contemporary writers, many women living in different parts of the world continue in this tradition by choosing a poetic format to communicate and to tell stories.

The writers, women living in Canada, the United States, Sri Lanka, Pakistan and India, were born in any of the above or in Africa, the Caribbean, Latin America or Europe; are heterosexual, bisexual or lesbian; are able or capable; born to "low" or "high" caste/class; live with implicit or explicit patriarchal structures; are first or second generation Canadians; are in the various seasons of our lives. In our diversity, we share the world. One of the many common elements of our lives is resistance and rebellion, through which we are changing the world. We find our own ways and words of resistance and all are chosen/taken from real life situations, none may be judged according to here. Or there.

With the exception, perhaps, of Caribbean and African South Asian-Canadian women, a woman who can write, and then write in English, whether living in South Asia, Canada or elsewhere, is likely a woman of comparative privilege in her community. Issues of underprivilege and discrimination are not those of extreme poverty and if they do deal with poverty, the story is told from a sentient/visionary space, not from the reality of a lived experience. This is a systemic barrier that is certainly not overcome in this anthology.

Aurat Durbar challenges literary and social critic alike. The synthesis of many different cultures and languages has produced words, expressions and forms that we may be ill-equipped to appraise; the content and terms of reference are diverse and so might not fit any politically correct format evolved in one cultural/geographic reference/location. We may have to stretch the limits of pundit/*maulvi*/canon constructs of both a literary and socio-political nature.

I am honoured to be the one to put together this work, which brings our collective and individual voices to us, and to you.

— FAUZIA RAFIQ

SUNERA THOBANI

Homecoming

"THIS WAY, Mrs. James."

The icy whiteness of the ward made Shelly shiver.

Pulling a chair up to the bed, the nurse motioned for her to sit. Her father was not to be disturbed, she reminded Shelly, briskly rearranging the flowers Shelly had brought.

Lowering herself into the chair, Shelly reassured the nurse she would be quiet. She glanced at the figure lying on the bed. Startled, she rose up again. This man was not her father. Her father was a big, burly man, not this frail, still person. The hospital must have made a mistake. But it had been five years since she had seen him, and as she stared at the face, she realized that this man on the bed was indeed her father.

His face was pale, almost the same as the grey his hair had turned into. Gone was the shiny brown sheen which she had so hated. For years she had tried to scrub the same sheen off her own face. A constant reminder of her otherness, try as she might, she had been unable to erase it. She was cursed with this skin which set her apart. Alien. Immigrant.

The hated words. The brown sheen, not letting her forget for a minute who she was. Immigrant. Always an alien.

She sat down. The grey which had descended upon her father's face bore the clamminess of death. The vibrancy of the brown sheen had been obliterated only by the denseness of this pallid, deathly grey.

The tubes going into his mouth and nose made her nauseous. Glancing away quickly, she fixed her eyes upon the monitor above the bed. The breathing tube made a rasping sound every time he drew upon it.

It was only a matter of time, she told herself with a calm certainty. She hoped it would end soon. Of course she did not want him to die, she caught herself quickly. But if he was as ill as the doctor said, then the sooner it ended the better. For his sake.

The heart attack had been severe, there was little hope of recovery. Shelly had listened to the doctor's words unmoved. Everybody had to die one day.

The calm within her was surprising. She could feel nothing. She felt sad, she corrected herself. Anybody would feel sad at seeing another human being in this condition. She did feel some sadness. Surely?

"You can hold his hand," the nurse's voice broke into her thoughts.

Shelly looked at the dry calloused hand, visible as the nurse lifted the blanket. It lay outstretched, as still as the rest of the body. The nails were stained dirty yellow from a lifetime of smoking, the dry skin on the back of the palm was peeling. It reminded her of scales on the skin of a drying fish. Nothing in the world would make her take that hand into her own. She did not want to touch death, the thought repulsed her.

"I ... don't want to disturb him," she forced a weak smile.

"As you wish." The nurse walked away.

The news had come without warning, dragging Shelly out of her sleep. Charles had answered the phone.

"I'll book a flight first thing in the morning, honey," he had said.

Shelly had not thought about going at all. What was the point? The doctors would do whatever was necessary. But Charles had taken it for granted that she would want to go, and so go she did. And now here she was, sitting in a sterile ward, next to a sick man whom she neither knew nor understood — and had no desire to.

He had had no visitors, the nurse had told her.

A man stubbornly living within the fortress of his own self, incapable of reaching another living being. Who else would visit him? But of course she said nothing to the nurse.

Her mother had died two years ago, when Shelly had gone to Europe for the first time. The trip had been Charles' birthday gift to her. They had learnt about the death much later. Shelly had not gone home that time.

Home? Is that what she had just called it? She had not thought of it as "home" in years. It had never been anything other than the place where she had spent the empty years before Charles came into her life.

She smiled as she remembered their first meeting. Life had really begun then, the time before had no meaning, no value for her. After her marriage, Shelly remembered nothing of her previous life but the pain. A heaviness arising from her gut and filling her up inside so she could feel nothing but the dead weight of it. It left her heart untouched, this weight she had carried around. There had never been a time when the pain had not been with her.

The never-ending battles between her parents.

"None of your brothers drink! I was stupid enough to marry the only man in your family who is a total failure."

"Oh yes! As if any of the others would have had you! Not a day goes by without you bitching about something or the other."

All her brothers were successful and Shelly's mother cursed the day she had married her father.

"And who turned me into a failure, tell me!" He would lash out. "Any other woman would know how to care for her family, how to make ends meet without sending me begging to my boss for an advance every month!"

"Yes, yes!! As if you earn enough for a family to live on. I swear, if it were not for the girl, I would have gone back to my brothers years ago!"

"Go then. Who's stopping you? Go and see if they will keep you for even one day!"

Inevitably, both turned on Shelly, the ultimate cause of their wretchedness.

"I suffer all this for your sake," her mother would scream at the child.

Her father said it was for her sake they had come to this miserable country. "Otherwise, why should we live here like dogs, far away from our own people?"

Shelly was sick of hearing how much it cost them to raise her, how much they had to sacrifice for her. Not that she could ever see what it was they were giving her. The house was a filthy, stinking hole. Always cold and damp. Nobody cared about anything. She planned to get away from it as soon as she could. And she had, as soon as she met Charles. She had gone far away, so far away that they could never reach her. Now she had a home for herself. Her life lay in front of her. With Charles.

Shelly glanced at the clock. She had been in the ward for almost two hours. There was no sound except the rhythmic gasping of the tube. The nurse was busy writing.

Tired, Shelly motioned to the nurse that she was going out to get something to drink. Sipping her coffee, she wondered how long it would be before she could go back. Charles would be waiting for her. They were going to visit his parents for Christmas, and she still had to buy gifts for everyone. This intrusion was very unfortunate; her father could not have found a worse time to get ill.

She loved Christmas with Charles' family; it was the only time of the year they spent together. There was always lots to eat and drink, all the things which her parents had never been able to afford. Charles' mother spent months preparing for this week, buying only the best for her family.

His family seemed to have accepted Shelly readily enough, even though Charles was the first in their family to have married a woman who was not white.

But there was something in the air that Shelly could never quite put her finger on. She never quite felt that she belonged. It was difficult to put this feeling into words. Perhaps it was the silence between them. The words which remained unsaid created a strangeness, a sense of quiet, unspoken distance which never seemed to dissipate. Everybody was polite. Too polite.

Maybe they felt it too, although Shelly was never sure of this. She sensed a certain awkwardness sometimes. Charles' mother asked her questions, but she never slowed down enough to listen to the answers. She would continue fussing around the house, cleaning after Shelly as if everything had to be wiped spotless again and again.

Charles' father never addressed her directly, it was as if he were speaking to a shadow standing behind her — hesitatingly as if unsure whether the shadow actually existed or whether it was his imagination.

"Darling, you have to understand how different their lives

are. Of course they love you, but they are from an older generation. They see the world differently, that's all." Charles taught her to be more understanding.

After that, it became easier to accept the long silences, with everybody engrossed in their own, sometimes unreachable, worlds. Charles disappeared for hours with the books he had not had time to read during the year. His mother baked and cooked, insisting Shelly not trouble herself with helping. Charles' sister went off to visit friends. Once Shelly got to know their ways, she learnt to appreciate the silences and to value the sense of family which brought them together this one time of the year.

Christmas became a time when she could eat and drink well. She could go for long walks along the beach, learning to value her solitude, knowing that Charles was only a few steps away.

Finishing her coffee, Shelly headed back to the ward. It might all be over by the time she got there. She missed Charles; she could almost smell his pipe. She loved the smell of that tobacco engulfing her as she sat in his study late at night. His study was her favourite part of the house. Sometimes she thought she could spend her life sitting there, watching him, waiting for him to look up and smile. She wanted to be with him now, not in some cold, sterile hospital ward.

"Any change?"

The nurse shook her head.

Sitting down, Shelly chided herself. She should have picked up something to read. The chair was uncomfortable, and as she shifted her weight, it scraped the floor. The nurse glared furiously, motioning her to be quiet. Angered by the sharpness of the gesture, Shelly bit her lip, forcing herself to sit still.

The nurse's gesture had spoken volumes. It was the same gesture Shelly remembered from school, from being treated like a child who could not entirely be trusted to behave herself. The feelings of humiliation from those young days were so unpredictable, rising to the surface across the distance of her youth.

Shelly had felt that same sense of humiliation on her way here. The flight attendant had served her a meal on the plane, banging the tray down in front of Shelly's face. Shelly had forced a "thank you," watching as the flight attendant smiled and chatted with the other passengers. It was always the same when she was without Charles. With him, everything was different.

An unexpected question gripped her mind. If the nurse was so curt with her, how had she treated her father? What could it have been like for him, alone, unable to breathe? A sharp pain ripped through Shelly's heart. She had never thought of her father in this way.

Shelly had asked the flight attendant for a drink on the plane. She had waited for the remaining two hours of the flight — the drink had never come. Now she wondered whether her father had asked for something which had not been brought to him. She brushed the thought aside. It helped nobody to think like that. She was getting tired. It would all be over soon, and she could go back to Charles. She would be warm again.

As evening turned into night, her heart ached. Earlier, she had thought that she could catch the evening flight home. Once this was all over, there was no reason for her to stay. But it was getting too late now to catch that flight. She would have to spend the night here.

The hours dragged on.

The city lights began to twinkle outside. In the darkness of the ward, Shelly tried not to think of anything. After a while, she managed to doze off.

Waking up with a start, Shelly realized she was very cold. A cup of coffee would help. The nurse followed her out.

"Mrs. James, these keys were in your father's pocket when he was brought in." She handed Shelly a bunch of keys on an old rusty piece of metal wire twisted into a ring. "You'd better keep them."

"Thank you." Unsure what to do, Shelly stuffed them into her pocket.

The cafeteria was closed. She walked over to the coffee machine in the lobby. Once there however, she decided against it. Coffee from the machine would taste stale. Deciding instead to go for a walk, she left the building. A walk would be refreshing, it would help her get through the night.

The cold brisk air was invigorating, giving her a burst of energy. The full moon lit the night sky, its rays sinking softly into the silent streets. Enjoying the warmth spreading through her body, she kept walking. After some time, she became aware that she recognized the streets. Here was the grocer's shop, and turning right at the crossroads, she saw the old school building. Somehow she had walked into the neighbourhood of her childhood, and there, only two blocks away, was their old house. Her father's house, she corrected herself.

She had better turn back, Shelly thought, she had walked much too far. She should have paid more attention to where she was going. But the house was so close now, why not go and see it? No, she decided.

It would be a shame to be so close and yet not see it, a voice inside whispered. It would not hurt to see it. Only from the outside, for just a moment, Shelly thought. Just to see if it was still as she remembered it.

Outside the house, she found herself reaching for the keys. In an instant, the front door was open. The familiar sounds of the house greeted her. The bottom stair still creaked as it had many lifetimes ago, and the latch on the door still squeaked. It had needed to be replaced even then.

Inside, the house was empty. Shelly walked from room to room. Nothing to greet her, only the dust and the silence. As she walked into the big bedroom, she saw that only the bed and the old trunk remained. What had happened to the other things? The dressing-table had left its marks on the carpet, as had the chest of drawers where her mother had kept her clothes.

Had her father sold everything after her mother's death? But why? Surely not for the money? He had always spent too much on his drinking and smoking. How Shelly had hated him smoking around the house! The stink of the cigarette smoke would linger in her hair forever. Money had been hard back then, he did not earn much working on a construction site. Her mother had worked too, minding other people's children, sometimes cleaning out offices at night. But they had managed. Why would he have sold everything now? Just like him to get rid of everything as soon as her mother was gone! He never thought of anybody but himself.

He should have let her know if he needed money; Shelly wiped away the angry tears momentarily stinging her eyes. But what if he had asked her? Shelly could not trust herself to answer the question.

Her eyes fell on the old trunk. Belonging to her grandmother, her mother had brought it with her in marriage. The paint on the outside was faded, the writing on it illegible even when her mother first got it.

The trunk was the only thing her mother had held on to in this country, not parting with it even in their hardest times. She had kept her most valued belongings in it. Her wedding sari, her silver jewellery, some old coins.

Shelly's happiest memories were of her mother opening the chest for airing. She would watch as her mother brought out the precious contents, unwrapping them one by one and setting them down gently, tenderly. The wedding sari had been Shelly's favourite. The deep red looked like it had been washed in a sea of fresh blood, the gold embroidery brilliant as the rays of the early morning sun. Touching the sari, the little girl dreamt of times spent in the glory of the gold woven through the rich old silk, giving it its magical quality. The old sari never lost its beauty for the little girl who pleaded with her mother to let her wear it for just a little while. Sometimes her mother would relent, letting her feel the rich silk against her body.

Now Shelly walked over to the trunk.

She opened it, not knowing what she would find inside. It was empty. All her mother's valued possessions gone. Stunned, she sat down.

Reaching towards the lid to shut the trunk, Shelly spotted something lying deep at the bottom. Her hands felt something soft, wrapped in wrinkled brown paper. Hoping it was the sari, she lifted it out. Maybe her father had cared enough to save it.

Unwrapping the old brown paper, she saw it was not the sari. A sudden flood filled her eyes, blurring her vision. Her fingers traced the embroidery on the *shalwar kameez* her mother had made for her daughter's wedding many ages ago. The brilliant sheen on the red silk darkened as the drops fell from her eyes.

Her mother had embroidered it when Shelly had reached puberty. Saving a bit of money every week, she had finally saved enough for both the material and the gold thread.

Charles had bought her wedding dress the day before they were to be married. Shelly would never have worn that gaudy embroidered thing. It was too garish.

She had stopped wearing *shalwar kameez* since high school, it was the only way she could stop the other kids from teasing her. She would never have worn that suit for her wedding.

It was many years later that Shelly had started wearing *shalwar kameez* and saris again. Charles liked her in them. She looked different, he said, made him proud of her. She made him feel special, different from his other colleagues at their annual dinners.

How long she sat in the dark, her fingers stroking the silk, Shelly did not know. Dawn was breaking over the city when she finally left the house.

Back in the ward, her father's condition remained unchanged. As she sat down, a nurse she had not seen earlier came and furiously motioned her outside.

"What do you think you are doing in there?"

"I'm visiting him."

"I have instructions to let in only one visitor," the nurse snapped. "Maybe you don't realize the seriousness of his condition. He is allowed no visitors."

"I'm his daughter."

"I'm sorry, you'll have to leave immediately."

"But ... I'm his daughter!"

"Sorry, only a Mrs. James is allowed to visit."

Shelly was afraid her head would explode with the anger pounding inside her.

"I am Mrs. James," she said with icy fury.

"I ... I ... I'm sorry," stammered the nurse. "Of course you can stay."

Shelly went back in, her face on fire. Why did she care so much? She should not get upset, Charles said. People make mistakes.

"And you must admit, honey, you don't look like the typical Mrs. James," he would tease.

She had hated her father's name, Janmohamed. At school, they called her Jammyhead. Even the teachers could not spell her name right: Shahsultan Janmohamed. "Shah of tan," "slave sultan," "jam 'n' bread" was what she got used to. Until she told friends her name was Shelly. Even Charles didn't know Shelly was not the name given to her at birth.

To be called something simple like "Mrs. James" had been her dream. But even in becoming Mrs. James, she still had to work hard to find the refuge she had sought. It was only with Charles that people accepted her as "Mrs. James."

What of her father, how did he cope with the ridiculing of his name? Had it been as hard for him?

Shelly understood for the first time how much harder it must have been for him. All the English he knew he had learnt here. But he had started working as soon as they had arrived. So had her mother. How had they coped with the humiliation of everyday life in this country? Shelly spoke English effortlessly. Embarrassed by her parents, she had wished many times that they wouldn't speak in front of her friends. Finally, she had simply stopped going out with her parents. Their accent was all wrong, she was all wrong when she was with them.

Had every humiliation found a home in her father's heart, as they had in hers? Was the pain etched upon his heart, engraved in his soul, as it was in hers?

The tears rolled down her face as he lay there silently, defying death, yet turning away from life.

For the first time in years, Shelly prayed. Do not let him die. She did not know who she was praying to, but she was pleading desperately for his life. She cried quietly, trying to ease the scorching flood behind her eyes.

The hours went by. She dozed, exhausted, every muscle and bone aching with fatigue, every corner of her heart weeping. Minute by agonizing minute, morning turned into afternoon; still he did not move, immobilized, caught in the moment between life and death. She awoke, her eyes wet, praying, until defeated by tiredness once more. She dozed again, shifting uncomfortably between the exhaustion of wakefulness and the empty solace of sleep.

And yet her father lay there. Still. Unyielding.

The doctor came; there was no hope her father would last the night, he told Shelly.

She refused to leave her father's side. Neither the doctor nor the nurse could persuade her to take a break.

She watched him, willing him to wake up. She pulled on every bit of energy in her body, directing it to his, hoping against hope. He had to open his eyes, she told herself. Nothing changed. Exhausted, Shelly leaned back.

The blanket, moved while the doctor was examining her father, now exposed his lifeless hand. She looked at the upturned palm, the skin coarse and hard from the labour of a lifetime. The cuts on the fingers, healed now but having left their scars, bore testimony to the harshness of his life. The skin was leathery, tough, as Shelly reached out and touched it. So different from Charles' hands. He had no cuts on his palms. No bruises, no marks. Charles was proud of them, the long, graceful fingers, well cared-for.

As she felt the tough skin of her father's palm, Shelly felt nauseated at the thought of Charles' soft hands on her body. Charles was like his hands. Soft. Graceful. Protected. Her father was like his hands, hard work in a struggle for survival which had turned skin into leather. A strong, rough exterior had covered his heart as surely as the coarse, hard skin had covered his hands. Hands which had sweated and bled all his life.

The tears rolled down Shelly's face. She gripped her father's hand; he could not go now. He could not leave her alone. Not now.

As she clung to his hand, she felt his fingers move. Shelly's heart stood still as she tried to stop the tears. Yes, he was squeezing her hand. She stood there, unable to speak, unable to do anything but cling to his hand.

"Mrs. James, your husband is on the phone." The nurse came up just then. "He wants to know if you will be going back today."

"Tell him I have come home," Shelly replied through the tears.

This War Is Declared

a war on women
they say
and claim
it is a war undeclared

women know otherwise

fearing the night
... the day
heads pounding
bodies broken
spirits weeping
taste of blood in mouths
and the claim ringing in ears
this war is undeclared

prisoners of war
within the confines of our own
homes lives hearts
they tell us
it is undeclared

the war
has been declared
every day
with every kick bite punch slap fuck shot stab
with every wound seen ...
and unseen ...
the war is being declared

esteemed judge asks
did he mean to kill?
forcefully confining her ...
violating her ...
placing wire around her neck ...
tightening it ...
she can't breathe ...
plastic bag over her head ...
beyond a doubt judge cannot tell
if the man really meant to kill
this war is declared

stripped and tied down ...
he shoves red-hot pepper into her ...
eleven convictions already ...
threatens to kill her
as soon as she lands ...
Immigration Officers say she is no refugee
this war is declared

her life destroyed ...
father wanting to play strange painful games in the night ...
since age three ...
for twelve long hard continuous years ...
no feelings inside her ...
she says it's as if she is dead inside ...
nothing moves ...
he gets four years
a declaration of war

found dead on a highway ...
face eaten away by animals ...
nameless faceless in death ...
it's her culture, they say
these bloody backward immigrants ...
what can the police do with these people ...
the community does not come forward with killer's name
police drop the case
it's a community affair they say
this war is declared

blasts her open ...
how dare she defy him ...
his honour demands her death
rumblings about cultural sensitivity warrant front pages
striving to understand his motives ...
desiring to understand his motives ...
an entire community of women is warned
WE WILL UNDERSTAND his motives
this is no small war

to raise a storm in the desert
fighter pilots arouse themselves
watch pornographic films ...
condemning women and children to living hell ...
far far away
a tiny dot on the screen ...
camera zooms in ...
point of view of bomb ...
quickly zooms out again
to catch surgical precision of explosion
this war rains from the skies

in every home street school office
inside ... outside
upside ... downside
supported by the forces of every land
this war is declared

this war is declared

and women know
this is no small
war

women know
rising in defiance
taking back the night
so we can have our day

SUDHARSHANA
COOMARASAMY

You Die but Once

At first it was our lands,
then it was our menfolk
who were maimed and slaughtered
to alienate and eliminate a culture
to hunt down and humiliate our ethnicity.

When they tortured my beloved
before my eyes and tethered hands,
a part of me died.
When they burnt my father alive
and ordered my mother to gather his ashes,
another part of me died.
When the Army hounded my brother
and left his butchered body at our doorstep,
another part of me died.
When they bulleted my little son

his heart-rending cry froze me to death.
When my frozen gaze registered my twelve year old
  daughter
being bled to death by manly brutality,
I felt my heart miss several beats —
reminding me that somewhere in me was life.

Gasping, I grasped at that last breath,
gathered it close and clung to it.
I crawled and hid and stole —
that gem, that gift, that grenade.
With all my might I threw
aiming at those men turned monsters.
The light that lit the sky
lightened my burden — a little
for thank God I felt no more.
I had died my death at last.

Armed Future

Infants trained to become infantry
weaned from the breast are
introduced to the bomb;
out of the womb and into war,
holding guns with two-way barrels
killing and being killed.
Maiming and being maimed.
Men, movements, visions of victory,
creating mirages of liberation
or the long-awaited self-determination.

Fed and filled with patriotic passion
unhesitantly exterminating elements,
fighting and dying for a cause —
superseding all other bonding.
forced conscription claiming not only women & men
but also our should-be blooming children.
Mothers we are, rendered barren,
robbed of motherhood, stilled and sterile.

Yet theorists theorize
that our future is in the hands —
in the hands that now hold
AK-47s, RPG-7s and M-16s.
What if the hands that hold the future
are blown to smithereens
and are stilled to silence,
and our future dies in infancy —
at the hands of the infants in infantry.

*The United Nations has estimated that there are 200,000
children under the age of fifteen bearing arms around the world
today. (Time, June 18, 1990)*

Now

("Till death do us part")
I don't want to waste a lifetime
waiting for my release.
I want to end a farce
that has already eaten up a decade.
My life — of what is left
I'd like to fill with joy
feel every moment
explore every dream.
I don't want to wait —
five or ten years more.
I want to end the farce
that's eating up my soul.
I want to save and salvage
of what is left of me.
Preserved in this morgue,
pampered by empty traditions,
dead I feel day long.
To sweet youth I bade adieu
centuries ago — or so it seems.
To live I don't want to wait
another century of pretence.

Either courage or cowardice holds me back
through the umbilical cord.
Tethered to the pulley of duty
I am pulled and pushed
wanted and rejected
in the single-same motion of life.

MAYA KHANKHOJE

The Transistor Radio

THE HOUSE WAS A LOVELY bungalow in Civil Lines, the former domain of British civil servants. As was the case with all buildings of that period, its architecture was a hybrid engendered by English common sense and the imperatives of a tropical climate. Its white-washed walls and red tiles — against the backdrop of a luxuriant garden — gave the bungalow a peaceful country air. Everything had been taken carefully into account: the verandah surrounding the rooms, the faded straw ceiling that kept the summer heat out, even the yard, the focal point of the household routine.

Tara Bai was squatting in the courtyard, near the *tulsi*, the small fragrant bush sacred to the Hindus. She was picking the little pebbles that sometimes found their way into the rice sacks. For this, she used a large flat basket in which she sifted the rice with the same rhythmical movements that her mother had taught her. Tara Bai felt soothed, as soothed as when she listened to the daily routine. Today, however, she wasn't lost in reverie. Today she was afraid.

"Tara Bai!" broke the shrill voice of Quentine, her mistress.

"Right away, Memsahib," answered Tara Bai.

"Did you get the yogurt ready?"

"Not yet, Memsahib."

Tara Bai dragged herself to the kitchen. She mixed a spoonful of yogurt in a bowl of warm buffalo milk and put it out in the sun so that it could start curdling. A few minutes later she was back at her previous task.

May the gods never find out! Her love for him, her husband, the gentle teenager she met on their wedding night, filled her with shame and made her blush. She was twelve then and he was thirteen. She had a vivid memory of her deflowering. No pain, but then again, nothing else. Later on they laughed when he confessed his ignorance.

Ashok, her beloved husband, her only friend. Deep down, she called him by his name, although she never pronounced it out loud. She had been taught not to tempt the fates by uttering his name. Thus the evil spirits could not touch him.

She was now thirty-two and he was thirty-three. Young still, but with a grandchild. No son. Merely two girls and the bittersweet memory of an infant son whose life faded two hours later. And now they want to meddle in their affairs. How can they understand? Most of them have children who can carry on the family name. But what about Tara Bai and her husband! Who will look after them in their old age? Who will light their funeral pyre? Who is going to ease their passage to another life? Without her realizing it, a big teardrop slid down her nose to drown in the rice sack.

As a rule, Tara Bai would go back home at sunset. However, tonight it was already dark when she crossed the threshold of their hut. Which was a shame, since Tara Bai loved to dawdle in the garden of the main house on her way home.

Ashok had already bathed and sat on the floor, near the door. He was drinking a tumbler of sugar-cane juice.

"The mistress has scolded you once again," he said gently.

"Of course not! She's very nice," said Tara Bai, slightly offended.

"You were weeping."

"Leave me alone! I must put the rice to boil and prepare the gravy for the *dal*."

"You were weeping," he persisted.

"Yes, I was, I hate her!"

"But you've just told me that she is very nice!"

Tara Bai stared at her husband stupidly.

"Nice? Who?" she finally asked. "Oh, no, I wasn't thinking about Canteen memsahib. I was thinking about her, up there, with her mighty airs."

"There you go again. The same old thing. Can't your female brain run around other circles?"

Having said this, Ashok strode out of the room and slammed the door. When he returned, he found supper all ready and served on a brass *thali*. This time she had added a little bit of mango chutney. He realized that this was by way of an apology.

"My dear wife," he said tenderly, "you are thinking about our infant son, aren't you?"

Her nod was barely perceptible.

"Well then, the gods lent us our baby boy for an instant and the gods took him away from us. Who are we to judge?"

"It's true," demurred Tara Bai. "But ... couldn't we have another one?"

Ashok looked at the melancholic face of his wife and told himself she was beautiful, in spite of her work-roughened hands, in spite of her enduring stubbornness. He put his hands on his wife's shoulders and said,

"Did you not know, my wife, that Indiraji made sterilization compulsory for government servants who have several children? God helps those who help themselves. If we co-operate with the government, the government will do like-wise. What's more, there are incentives, such as a transistor radio, a day off...."

"But it's unfair!" she cried out indignantly. "The gods have not yet bestowed a son upon us!"

"Yes, yes, I know. But you haven't conceived in ten years!"

"Then why get sterilized at all!"

"Because one never knows!" he said impatiently.

"In that case I might wind up having a son!"

Ashok smiled at his wife's water-tight logic.

"Besides," she added timidly, "we are still young and it is not a sin."

Ashok approached his wife and slowly undid the coil in the nape of her neck. He caressed her hair longingly and whispered to her ear,

"Yes, we are still young, my little star. But you know, it is just a question of a needle prick. A man does not cease to be a man for that. The doctor explained it all at the meeting. And I have spoken to Moti Lal. He says it's true. Don't be afraid, little one."

The following day was Easter. Quentine had cooked an elaborate meal for the whole family and her friends. Easter was like Holi, when Hindus welcome spring. This year, Easter and Holi almost fell on the same days due to the lunar calendar. It was easy for Tara Bai to identify with Easter. When Christians paint eggshells with gay colours, Hindus spray bright dyes on each other's clothes. Those vivid colours on spotless white looked ever so nice! And the merry tipsiness of the guests at the main house reminded Tara Bai of the effects of almond milk laced with *bhang*. Unfortunately, the government forbade the use of *bhang*, that ordinary herb whose effects were so extraordinary! The government again! Anyway ...

If Christians could celebrate the resurrection of a dead Christ, why couldn't Tara Bai invoke life back into a hollow womb! This time, she was in charge of pouring tea. In moments such as these, her feeling was one of well-being, almost joy. She placed the tea tray and the cups on a low table in the livingroom. On another tray, she laid out cucumber sandwiches, little sweatmeats and onion *bhajies*.

"But my dear Quentine," was saying John to his sister, "it's not at all the same thing! If you want more children that's quite understandable. And your husband can certainly afford it. And these days children will grow up to become upright citizens who'll help the country. But someone like your maid, that's preposterous!"

"John, be quiet," murmured Quentine nervously. "She understands English."

"My dear," went on John, "even if she were to understand — and between you and me, I doubt it — she ought to know that it's sheer folly for her to bear a child at her age."

"She is my age," said Quentine icily.

"Is that so? Well, Indians just age faster. Where was I? Ah, yes, I can't take it up with the Health Minister. After all, my professional reputation is at stake."

"Quentine," said Peter to his wife, "if a Catholic can defy our beloved Church on the issue of birth control, don't you think your dear friend could accept her husband's vasectomy? If it were up to me, I would have them all sterilized!"

Tara Bai felt a lump in her throat and she left the room abruptly. Quentine saw this and ran after her.

"Tara Bai, look at me!"

Tara Bai covered her face with the border of her sari. She was ashamed to weep in front of her mistress.

"Tara Bai, don't be afraid. Since my husband and my brother refuse to help you, we'll do things my way. Do you remember Ahmad Khan, my brother's chauffeur? Well, I'm sure with a little gift we can convince him to undergo the operation in your husband's place. We'll take care of the paperwork. But do take it easy. This is my Easter gift to you."

Tara Bai burst into sobs.

"Aren't you pleased, Tara Bai?" Quentine asked gently.

"Thank you, Memsahib, but ... Ahmad Khan isn't even married." Quentine couldn't hold back her laughter.

"Of course he's not married. Haven't you heard what they say about him?"

"I understand," said Tara Bai slowly. "He already has children."

"Of course not, silly little one! He is rather strange, you see, he ... anyway, he treats all women like sisters, if you know what I mean."

Tara Bai blushed. Then very slowly she went down on her knees and touched her mistress' feet.

"May the gods bless you," she murmured.

All of a sudden, with a very broad smile on her lips, she ran through the courtyard, through the garden, past the well, till she reached her hut. There she stopped short. Her husband was lying on the bed. He was fiddling with a small Zenith transistor radio. A sweet woman's voice was singing "... please allow me to seek refuge under the shadow of your eyelashes ..."

"Did you take off for Easter? Are you ill? Who gave you the radio? Answer me!" she cried out in panic.

Ashok sat up and put the radio to her ear.

"Nice, isn't it? They say it sells for rupees 250 — in the black market."

Tara Bai stared at her husband, her eyes wide open with horror. She stepped back. Her lips quivered. A lump in her throat. She suddenly felt sick and her ears started ringing.

She began twisting the end of her sari without realizing it.

"What's the mater with you, woman! You're never pleased! Look at me, the head chauffeur!" And saying this, he held his wife's face between his hands. "No more night duty, no more botheration! And a few extra rupees to boot!"

Tara Bai was shocked, silenced.

"You know," he said coaxingly, "we could save money and go to Benares, to the Ganges, on a pilgrimage."

Tara Bai's features suddenly hardened and with a purposeful stride she walked out of the room.

"... besides," Ashok mumbled, "it was just a tiny needle-prick...."

Did I Ever?

did i ever say
that i could
find you
in her arms
and not really
care?

i did

did you truly believe
that her arms
would not
strangle
my love
for you?

you did

were we ever
young
and foolish
and true believers
in love and
all that jazz?

i don't remember

did you really think
that you could
take on the world
while i stoked
the fires
at home?

now really!

you
silly
man

The Watershed

MANY PEOPLE aspire to a ripe old age, but when they reach it they spend most of their efforts denying it. For others, age is so irrelevant that they do not even know how old they are. Some measure their lives not chronologically but in terms of achievements.

Nina Berberova was first published in her eighties and she is now the talk of literary salons. During his brief life Mozart found time to create a legacy of beauty for us to enjoy. Christ sacrificed his life at the age of thirty-three for us to learn the meaning of our own. Does age matter? Not really. Age is just a marker from a point called birth and another one called death in the continuum that is known as life. It stands to reason that living life fully is more important than measuring it.

Most people in the industrial world live out their biblical three score and ten. Many in the third world do not make it past childhood due to hunger, disease, war, the cruelty of the human species, or the simple alienation of the modern world. Statistics vary.

I'm one of the lucky statistics. By turning fifty last year I more than beat the odds faced by the average Indian born in 1942, whose life expectancy was about thirty-seven. I'm too old perhaps to change my career, not old enough to retire, the right age to become a grandmother and young enough for a partner.

In fact, my daughters might be horrified to learn that I entered a contest in which "winning would mean losing" because then everybody would know my real age. Why would I want to proclaim my age to the four winds? And why not? After all, why withhold my age from a friend or a lover when my banker, the government, my employer and a host of other strangers know it? I am as proud of my age today as I was when young and as I hope to be when truly old.

Especially if I get to earn the title of lovely old lady, lovely as in full of love.

Age, of course, is a social construct as much as a fact of life. Ageing well means wearing life like a warm, beautiful and useful garment and then shedding it lightly, when the time comes. My Indian father, who was born in a culture that values the elderly, died at eighty-two, a picture of his family under his pillow and a peaceful smile on his lips. I aspire to die like him but for that I will have to live like him as well.

He showed me how youth and age can coexist in one body; how the body is the temple of the soul and therefore deserves respect; how it is necessary for mind, body and soul to work in harmony. Since he was already old when I was born I was aware of how briefly his light would shine on us, so one morning when I found him standing on his head, I chided him for endangering his health. His retort was that he had been doing yoga all his life and that it was the first time in mine that I had got up early enough to see him do it.

From him I also learnt that whereas the past informs your life, it is the future that provides it with inspiration. At eighty he didn't consider himself too old to add another language to the many he already spoke, or to contemplate a perilous journey, even if it was only in his imagination.

Youth believes in the myth of immortality. Old age destroys that myth. At the watershed age of fifty I no longer believe in myths. My imagination is fired by the secrets that nature chooses to reveal to us and intrigued by those that the human soul tries, not always successfully, to withhold. As for my soul, it awaits release without a sense of urgency.

As I look out my window at the frozen landscape, I smile at the certainty that come spring, the rose will bloom.

And if it does not, it is because it is time for the land to lie fallow.

SHAHNAZ STRI

My Hands

Look at my hands.
Brown hands
with slender fingers,
a ring on my small finger.

I look on the inside —
lines of life everywhere —
there are no scars here,
no evidence left
of damage done.

My hands.
I look at them every day,
I cry and scream into them,
they scratch the itch of pain away,
they write my words.
They hold me tight —
when no one is around,
keep me together as I fall apart.

These hands have no eyes,
no mouth no voice,
yet I see so much with them.

See my hands
as they draw pictures of heads
with no bodies
It is not necessary for them.

They draw pictures of confusion,
with nothing to say,
they draw my words into anger.

My hands
are mine —
they will do,
what I cannot say.

MINA KUMAR

There Is No Place Like Home

YOU DO IT WHEN you are pregnant. You don't know whether
hormonal imbalances due to pregnancy have made you crazy
or whether having the possibility of a child inside you makes
you crave the possibility of a mother. You are careful to call
it "possibility of a child." You are still not sure what you are
going to do about the whole situation. The man — for that
is all you can bring yourself to call him, and if people ask
what man, you point to your stomach — the man is not
much help. He is in general not much of anything but you
are fairly certain that your mutual offspring would have
frizzy hair and this appeals to you greatly. This kind of atti-
tude is definitely inherited from your mother, which is
another reason she is on your mind.

You haven't done it in six years. It has never really
occurred to you except as idle fancy. You haven't wanted to
any more seriously than you have wanted to be a blonde. It's
one of those things to think of in an idle moment, and no
more.

This whole thing does not derive just from matters of the womb. Your paternal aunt, Padmini, has called your father who has called you to inform you that your stepfather has called your aunt five times to get her to tell you to call your mother. You laugh. Why should you bother? You are convinced that you will not do something so stupid as drag mess back in your life. Your mother is mess. It is an equation. Then your life gets messy all on its own. You are pregnant. You have lain in bed for a week. Your home pregnancy test is still lying on the dining table. Half-eaten delivered food and half-read newspapers and dirty clothes litter the floor. You haven't left your apartment in a fortnight. You have missed your mid-terms. You vomit every time you eat and you have diarrhea. You have a headache. The smell of most anything makes you ill. You think incessantly about death and you are afraid of drowning in the shower. Your vagina leaks constantly. Your sheets are filthy. Your hair is greasy and matted. You are tired of wandering the city unmoored and alone. The man does not call you and you crave being next to him and you hate him. You are tired of not having anyone to notify in case of emergency. You are tired of not being sure who will stand by you if something goes wrong. You want a place to lay your hat because there is no place like home.

You turn the TV off. You sit up in your bed. You retie your ponytail. You pull the phone to you. Its back is streaked with dried bolognese sauce. You grope the pile of newspapers and mail and homework on your end table for the right piece of paper. You feel reckless. You call your mother.

You want to ask her about the time when you were a child when you couldn't go to sleep at night because you were so afraid of dying. You want to tell her about the man who has made you pregnant — about all the others, too, but especially about this man. You remember how she said of your schoolgirl crush on Prince, "The attractive thing about Black men is that they are tall and broad-shouldered and you have to pick the one Black man on the planet who is a runt."

You want to tell her the man is tall and broad-shouldered. And you remember her telling you jokingly that you were luckier than she because you would have the opportunity to find out if what they said about Black men was true. And you want to tell her how angry the man was when you told him what she had said and you want to tell her how skinny his dick is. You want to tell her how wonderful you are, that you are going places and that you are somebody and that you will be more successful than she. And you want to tell her that you are pregnant.

You left your mother at fourteen. In your head, you call that time "that certain summer" and the memory smells of earth after rain. The first new night, lying on a mattress on the floor because the bed hadn't been set up yet, your feet resting against a cardboard box of books, you thought about that first kiss that hours later still made you feel like a balloon filled taut with radiance. You had pulled off your shirt and *churidar* and lay in a skimpy black leotard, running your hands over your lips, your neck, and those yet uncharted places: your breasts, your stomach, that moist, fragrant mystery between your legs. You ran over details over and over again, his lips, the sun, his tongue. You pulled the yellow sheet over your bare legs and listened to the first rains drumming past your open window. You were reborn.

You were no longer a child. Your mother ceased to seem a necessary part of yourself and you required her to appeal to you on an objective level.

Objectively, she did not appeal to you at all. It didn't matter. You descended the staircase the next afternoon to get some lunch, and when your mother didn't respond to your greeting, you barely noticed, still smiling. Your mother was making sandwiches, her neck bent, eyes focussed on the cutting board. Your step-brother said, "Good morning, Acca."

"Hey." You flopped down on a chair in front of the telephone. Your mother took the sandwiches and two glasses of juice out into the backyard. Your brother pattered out after her. You picked up the phone.

You would have called Robyn, but she lived in Kitchener and you couldn't make a long distance call. You called Nicole instead and opened the fridge. You pulled out the tub of butter. You took out four slices of brown bread. You made your lunch and told her all about Nicholas, what he was wearing, what his house looked like, the waffles his younger brother was eating.

Before your mother came inside, you scurried back up to your room and closed the door. You pulled out from your school bag a Françoise Sagan novel and you thought about love and passion and the fruits of the world that you would eat: green apples, peaches, cherries, pomegranates, Moroccan oranges, bland Haitian mangoes. You saw faces in the purple-flowered, green-leafed wallpaper on the wall of your new room and day dreamed and wrote stories about girls in love.

You read *La Chamade* and played Paul Weller singing "Paris Match." Grace gave you the tape as a present for your fourteenth birthday, which was that day. You paused between chapters. Would Nicholas remember, would he call? You reached up to your brother's Smurf tape player and rewound "Paris Match" again. You didn't know which box held your own tape player and this was not the right time to ask your mother. You lay flat on your back, the sheet tangled around your legs, your bare arms prickled with goose bumps.

"Empty nights with nothing to do I sit and think and every thought is for you."

That summer, you listened to "Paris Match" and read novels. There was no money to do anything else. You had just moved from Meadowvale to North York, so you didn't know anyone in the area to babysit for. The three dollars and fifty cents you had you soon spent. Asking your mother for your savings was pointless. She didn't even respond when you asked if you could go to the library. You found this bizarre, but you had other things to think about. You looked up the library's address in the phone book. You strolled out-side, and got directions at the street corner from the old Indian man who lived next door. When you discovered the library was closed, you went to the next door McDonald's and soon lost yourself in the grass behind the library in an orgy of apple pie and desire. His straw-coloured hair smelled like Ivory soap, his eyes ... his eyes required poems.

Feeling expansive with joy, you decided to go home and "make an effort." Only the screen door was closed because of the summer heat. Through the netting you could see everyone posed on the livingroom couch. You entered.

"Hi," you said. "Hi."

Your stepfather's eyes briefly met yours.

"Hi Acca!" your brother said, and the ebullience in his voice was so out of place that even he noticed and fell silent.

The teenager who lived across from you skateboarded past and the screech of the wheels resounded in your ears. Your mother did not turn.

They were playing a geography game and your mother continued, "There's another airport in London, isn't there? Heathrow and something else." You sat lightly on the arm of the couch behind her. The door to the backyard was also not closed. The sun was setting.

"I don't know," your stepfather said guiltily.

"Gatwick." Your voice was edgy. This was boring. His lips, his tongue, that sweetness.

"Gatwick," your stepfather said.

"Yes, Gatwick. That's what it's called," said your mother. You rose.

You mounted the stairs to your room. As night fell, you became hungry. All you had eaten that day was two McDonald's apple pies. You listened impatiently to hear their footsteps going up to the floor above you. Your mother slept in the master bedroom, your stepfather slept on a blanket in the rec room across from the master bedroom because he snored. Your brother still slept with your mother though he was six. His bedroom was across the hall from yours and it was empty.

Yours held a broken shelving unit stacked with paints, brushes, turpentine, nails and a set of screwdrivers, the frame of your bunk bed, a cardboard box; your stepfather had stored these items in your room as you lay sleeping.

You sat sideways on the pretty green-striped love seat so that you faced the wallpaper instead of the mess and finished La Chamade and played "Paris Match" and felt hungry. "I hate to feel so confined feel like I'm wasting my time."

You did feel confined but you knew you weren't really wasting your time. You thought of yourself as a caterpillar in a cocoon. You just didn't know what you were turning into, but you more or less patiently waited. As the weeks wore on, you began to evade your mother as much as possible. You didn't like feeling invisible. You did not want a confrontation. You leaned against the windowsill and listened for portents in the nights. It was one of the rainiest summers the Toronto area had ever seen and the gushing, wet nights were a wonderful time. After everyone had gone to bed, you descended the staircase from your bedroom into the kitchen and collected supplies for the next day. The things you ate had to be simple and storable because you never knew when you would get into the kitchen again, so you were converted to peanut butter sandwiches, *laddu*, apples, butter and aniseed on brown bread. You still vividly remember the intense tartness of pink lemonade and the rapture of grasshopper Oreo that summer. You listened to Sade. "Sweet as cherry pie, wild as Friday night." One day, though you didn't know how, you knew you would be wild as Friday night and if he looked good, you would hope he could dance.

Once, out of desperation for something to read, you went upstairs to the bookshelf of your mother's bedroom. It was forbidden to you, you guessed because of the sex manual about how to satisfy a woman. You had already read it in the library and discovered nothing you didn't already know. You gingerly tiptoed to the shelf and read the titles. Your mother and brother had gone out ten minutes earlier and there was no telling when they would get back. There wasn't much time to choose. You skipped the thrillers, the baby care book, the dictionary, your heart pounding. You eased out a copy of *Hollywood Wives*, and hurried back to your room.

Your mother was an intellectual, she had proclaimed many times. She had raised you an abridged versions of 19th century classics and told you what to disdain: religion, illiteracy, Muslims, low-brow entertainment. When you realized how well-thumbed and dog-eared the pages of *Hollywood Wives* were you felt a vague, stirring disappointment. Your mother didn't even believe in buying books because you could after all borrow them from the library, but she owned this book. You went from the opening urination to the finish in a couple of hours and lay in bed with nothing to do. You wanted to keep yourself occupied, not thinking about

Nicholas, who had made Robyn tell you he would not call. You picked through the box of books again. The only things you hadn't reread were an atlas of the human body and a crumbling copy of *Madame Bovary* that you bought in fourth grade because the cover was more appealing than the cover of *Paradise Lost*. You read it in a gulp. When Emma died, dawn broke and you cried. You were becoming a woman, so you were not just Heathcliff, but Emma, too.

You didn't know why your mother stopped talking to you after you moved to North York. Before the move, your relationship was at its usual pitch: unstable. Of course, you had long since regarded her good humour with suspicion, so you were on the receiving end of less and less of it and your stepfather and brother proportionally more, but your attentions were elsewhere, so you didn't really notice if the tenor of your relations changed. After the weekend they moved and you were in Kitchener with Robyn, there was consistency in her response to you. You were met with silence.

But your heart was singing, so your ears were full of noise. "All You Need Is Love," which was his favourite song. "All Shook Up," which he sang into your ear after you kissed that first, sun-drenched kiss, his coarse, thick lips on yours. "You Spin Me Right Round (Like A Record)," which was playing on his TV when he took you home. "Frankie's First Affair" and "When Am I Going to Make a Living" and "Nothing Looks the Same in the Light" at night as you lay in bed, at night when you slipped into the kitchen to make emergency sandwiches, in the dawn as you fell finally asleep, thinking about just before where you now were, about Nicholas, further back to Robyn, the weekend right before Nicholas.

The weekend in Kitchener with Robyn, you lay on her bunk bed and fantasized about Antonio, and she about Jeff

Sloan. This is what you talked about. It is easy to remember because you taped your conversation for posterity. The man who put the possibility in your belly accidentally listened to the tape and was convinced that your only interest in life has been men. You didn't try to explain to him that you were not talking about what happened before you arrived at Robyn's house, about your mother handing you ten dollars and your new address and responding to your request for more precise directions with the word, "Fly." You didn't explain that it was almost your birthday and for your last birthday your mother had given you a pale yellow pantsuit and splashing, spreading pain across your face. You didn't explain that she had turned to your stepfather on seeing you dressed in the ill-fitting pantsuit and ill-fitting good cheer and said, "She should always be like this." You didn't explain that you were trying to find a way not to always be like that. You didn't explain, you hushed then and didn't explain and he cuddled you and you could pretend he was completely yours.

At the end of the weekend with Robyn, after making the tape and not discussing how you would go home, you gathered in the mall with Robyn and her friends Nicholas and Antonio and Todd and Jeff. You liked Antonio, Portuguese and dashing, but it was pale, blue-eyed Nicholas who said his mother would chauffeur you to your new residence. Afterwards, it all seemed quite odd, which is why Robyn laughed on first hearing the story from Nicholas and he became embarrassed at his venture and wouldn't speak to you again, but this was the way it happened. Somewhere between going to his house to meet his mother and arriving at your house, he told you he loved you. Of course it was funny — pale, shy Nicholas and dark, bold, noisy you. But your heart was awash in gratitude and you gazed into his eyes, yes, Flaubert, those eyes more limpid and more beautiful than the mountain pools in which the sky is reflected, and told him not to be jealous over Antonio and you kissed and you still remember the warmth of the sun and the radiance in your body as his tongue entered your mouth. Never mind that his mother was driving and no doubt could see all that was going on. No wonder Robyn laughed! Then Nicholas became embarrassed and told you to forget all that had happened. But how could you?

Instead, you wrote stories about girls in love and nodded knowingly on encountering Leon and wondered when you would meet Charles and Rodolphe. Now that you have lost your virginity to a Berber shepherd Charles, and you are pregnant by a Haitian, crummy Rodolphe, you wonder if it is time for the arsenic and are afraid to die.

That summer you were afraid of nothing. You leaned against the window and stared at the picturesque rowhouses along a snaking cobblestone pathway and tried to think rationally about what to do. You called social service agencies and gathered information about shelters for runaways. You were getting tired of not having shampoo or Kleenex or toothpaste. You either filched some from your mother's bathroom in small amounts congealed onto the dispenser cap or did without. Once, you overcame your distaste and awkwardness, and as your mother was walking across the landing, you opened your door and asked her to give you a stick of deodorant. She walked down the stairs and you wondered if you had actually said it or only thought of saying it and you watched her mass of curled hair, taut zebra-striped leotard and baggy red sweatpants disappear around the corner to the kitchen. You retreated.

That summer you washed your hair with a hoarded cake of Dove soap. You used rolled-up toilet paper as a sanitary napkin. You hadn't eaten cooked food in months. The fall was approaching and you had no idea where the local school was. You needed new shoes. The wavering could not continue and you knew you had to force a change. Nicholas' flicker of love had convinced you that you deserved better.

The next time you were in the house alone, you told Nicole and she said she would help, but when the time came, her mother said they were going out to dinner which they so rarely did and therefore couldn't you get someone else. Her father told you to make an effort and maybe things would go back to the way they were. You explained that the way things were was worse and it was the improvement from pain to silence that inspired you to improve your station even more. You packed two pink bags full of clothes and twelve cold-smelling pennies in your pocket and sat in a nearby McDonald's, watching other people eating and waiting.

Eventually, the police carted you home and asked you if you knew that you were a fool. Eventually, through an old teacher, you found your way to school. Eventually, you were assigned a social worker who was a former Moonie. You were not given keys to the house you had been returned to. Once, after coming home from the library, you found the house empty and locked, so you waited at the neighbour's for someone to come back, and thus incurred your mother's only sentence to you that summer, when she told you not to shame her by letting the neighbours know. Again, one day, you came back from school to again find the door locked and no one home. You went around to the back door, which you could jimmy open. Just as you entered, your mother came in through the door. She flew at you, her fists raised, for tracking backyard dirt into the livingroom. You raised your hand. You would like to think that you hit her but you missed. Still, what a moment it was, you springing out of the cocoon and out the door forever.

You spent a few nights in Isabella Street shelters for pros-
titutes and some years living in the house of an old, ugly
white woman with two adult sons and a great many Great
Danes. You cleaned the shit stains around their toilets and
the shit the dogs left and your life was endless shit. This was
the improvement. Then, having gotten your number from a
girl whose father was her husband's older brother, your Aunt
Padmini called you to wish you a happy birthday and
through this accident your father's money reentered your
life. Somehow, the climaxes in your life tend to involve your
birthday and/or your Aunt Padmini.

You sit staring at your mother's Aunt Padmini-derived
phone number scrawled on a sodden Bengal Café take-out
menu. In six years, there has been only silence and this
hasn't bothered you. At one time, when you were beginning
to trust an uncle's beautiful bride, between confiding your
lusts and your ambitions, you leaned over the kitchen
counter and told to her about your mother.

"I know," Vijaya responded, chopping up onions. "You
still love her." The onions sizzled as they plopped into the
sambar. You looked at her in horror. This was the beginning
of the crumbling of your respect for her. No one who puts
your life in such a position that you are scheming for toothpaste can be met with love, and you were under the impres-
sion that this was obvious. Curiosity or self-destructive
attention or corrosive anger, yes, but not love, not your rich,
cream and butter and plump raisins and vermicelli love. You
are waiting for a meritorious someone to nourish with this
paysam. You are looking for someone to trust. You are looking for someone for forever. You are looking for a home.

Though it's easy for you to forget when you rest your
head on his chest, the man who made you pregnant is not
that someone. He has told you that he is too busy — busy

dancing and drug dealing and drinking and playing domi-
noes. "You want your boyfriend to be your mommy and
daddy, and I'm not up to that," he said. "You're a child to be
having a child and I am not up to taking care of a wife and a
child." He wants to give your baby, if it's a boy, to his grandmother. If it's a girl, he informs you, you can flush it down
the toilet. His flicker of love, such as it was, has died out.

You are grateful when Aunt Vijaya tells you that you can
live with her if you decide to have the baby but you are tired
of accepting the kindness of strangers.

You have no idea how to deal with a baby on your own.

You don't know if you are ready to have a child. You are
afraid of your fears and rage, afraid they would surge out of
you like spikes and warp her. You are afraid because your
grandmother warped your mother who warped you and
maybe the poison is in the blood. Still, you have visions of a
girl child of three whose brown, frizzy hair you would braid.
This is utterly ridiculous because you and the man both have
black hair. But you hunger for your little girl. "Baby girl, my
baby girl," you say into your pillow.

You cup your belly, saying, "My baby girl." Your mother's
grandchild. Your round-cheeked baby girl. You tally yourself
and the man and conclude she would have a flattish nose and
big brown eyes and a golden brown complexion. You call
everyone who has seen both of you. "Do you think her hair
would be straight, frizzy or nappy?" you ask. "Do you think
she would like me?" you ask your friends. I will never hit
her, you say to yourself, sitting on a stool, staring at the pink
pregnancy test. And you make a mental list. Never let her
feel so lonely that she will cling to a Haitian drug dealer who
lies and steals and hits her. Play maths games with her. Tell
her she is beautiful. Buy her a frilly dress with a pink sash.
You wonder how you should explain her father to her. She is

the baby girl you have always known you will have, but you don't know if now is the time.

You guess that your father would still give you money. He has had six heart attacks and he says he wants a grandchild. In any case, your family has no doubt been expecting something of the kind for years. You resent confirming their expectations. You are apprehensive of the cloud this would create over your baby girl's life. You know this would mean that you would be taking your father's money for a lot longer than you have projected and this displeases you. You don't know if you have sloughed off your past enough to have a child. You don't know anything. You don't know what to do. You call your mother.

You are not thinking about her as a person. After all, it has been six years and you don't know who she is right now. You are thinking more of a generic mother. You are thinking of Michelle's mother who helped her get an abortion and took her temperature the next day and brought her Tylenol. You are thinking of Joyce's mother taking care of Joyce's niece. You are thinking of not wanting to be so alone that despite all that has happened you still crave being in the man's arms because that is the only calm you know. You are thinking of that Christmas Day in Astoria with a middle-aged, if half, Moroccan who, after you had both lost your virginities, had gone out for a jog, while you lay in the soiled, petal-strewn bed wishing you hadn't wanted it so badly and been so unsure you would get it, and wishing you had a mother to tell you not to throw yourself away on an illiterate, alcoholic Berber waiter from sheer ignorance that better individuals existed to love you. You are thinking of someone to remind you of your beauty. You are thinking of "a" mother. You are not thinking of your own.

Your mother brings to mind not the woman that she is

but food you ate when you were with her. You summon up visions of *porichche kute*, drumstick *sambar*, garlic *rasam*, beans *patani kute*, black chillies, real *thair, pushnika morqoy-ambe*, lemon *rasam, avial*, tomato *goche, mor rasam*, pumpkin *sambar, pdalanga sambar, avacka, covacka, pavacka*, things that you can't even say in English whose strong tastes your pregnant body craves.

Your mother is the only good cook you know. Deliveries from restaurants and Campbell's cream of celery soup and spaghetti à la Harold cannot satisfy these heady desires. You vomit your rigatoni bolognese. Your head is clouded with thoughts of sauces of bitter vegetables, sour vegetables, sharp vegetables. This is what you are thinking of.

You are not thinking of the time when you bumped into your mother and the pot of hot tomato soup slipped and scalded your back so the flesh sizzled and bubbled and you screamed, running up and down the room, screaming and your mother looked at you blankly and told you not to fuss, though she finally called the nurse who lived downstairs, who examined you accompanied by her children while you lay on the bed with your underwear pulled down, but it took so long to get something for the pain and you still have the burn that the nurse's son said was the shape of Australia on the small of your back. This is not what you are thinking of. Your mother is not who you are thinking of.

Your mother, that brilliant creature, who with a toss of her permed hair explained that her only flaw was her bad temper. Your mother, whose husbands past and present attest that she is an exemplary mother, epitome of beauty, intellectual luminary. Your light-skinned, pockmarked, uneven-toothed mother, the epitome of beauty, who told you from the age of seven that if you stayed fat, dark, slovenly, you would never get a man so that when an Algerian thief in Barcelona slid his hand in your pantyhose and said, "I think you have a complex about your body and I don't know why because you have a beautiful body," you cried ecstatic tears, your mother who bought the *National Enquirer* and said on watching the Oscars that she too could win one, this woman with two failed marriages and a daughter whose location she doesn't know and a son whom she kissed wetly on the mouth, who told you that all the proof you needed of her excellent mothering was that she introduced you to the Brontës and Dickens and comic books of Shakespeare's plays when you were nine.

You haven't thought of these things in years. What is there to think of them? Your mother, you tell those you meet, is dead. You like saying it. It simplifies. It is a mark of your respect and trust that you tell someone the truth. You were so taken with Marita that you spilled out the story the first night you lay together in bed. You told the man to try to make him understand you, but he replied that all parents discipline their children like that, and then he crossed his scarred arms over his face and went to sleep.

After you received the message to call your mother, the man told you he would like to meet her and shake her hand, and you hated him, purely and intensely, before your need overtook that emotion. He himself was thrown out of the house by his father because he was rude to his stepmother, so you try to restrain your judgement. You understand, because you also feel, the urge to sentimentalize other people's families.

Over the years, you whittle down your feelings about your mother to this: she was there, as opposed to your father, who has been a cipher, on and off with cash. It's not that you don't think you need mothering, but she has no relevance to that need. You are not calling because you expect it from her. You are calling because the growth in your uterus is making you, like Lot's wife, look back.

You call because all you know is the weakness you feel. It is an impulse that is fulfilled before it is considered, like being drunk and suddenly vomiting, and similarly brief. You get under the cheap Polyfill green comforter stained with food and your come. The light from the men's bathroom in the building opposite yours trickles over the bookshelf into darkness. The light in the phone is a faint yellow glow.

Your call lasts eight minutes, in which she commends your healthy self-esteem when you tell her you are in college, explains that she is not alive to be the librarian to your past, enquires of your goals for your relationship with her, informs you that she is not interested in recriminations, guilt trips, *balem*-allotting, dredging up the past, because good and bad are relative, admits she is into New Age philosophy and says she's not interested in your judgements, screams that she wants a civil, sharing relationship, responds, when you point out that she is screaming, that niceness isn't her strong point.

You decline the offer of a relationship and hang up the phone. You are stunned. Your mother is a New Age groupie! You are shocked. You are disgusted. This is worse than reading Jackie Collins. This is not what you expected. Your mother raised you on rationality and the scientific method so that you are now petrified of dying and are full of existential angst and she has become a New Age groupie. You are saddened. You realize that you will truly never talk to her again. You realize that you are really all alone, and you cannot inflict this on a child. As much as you liked the idea of braiding frizzy hair and of singing "*Thu mere saath rahenguan munne*" as you cup your swollen belly, you know that you have to wait to have your baby girl. You tell yourself again that you are all alone. You tell yourself you don't need to click your heels because there is no place that is home except inside you because home is where the heart is throbbing in your body and this body is your only real home. Then, feeling empty, you crawl under the dirty sheets and hug your pillow and dream of the day when this will no longer be true.

Archana Sharma

My Golden Brown Goddess

A YOUNG DAUGHTER cuts out a cube of her fleshy forearm and feeds her mother a soup of tissue and blood to bring her back from the land of the dead. This image assaults my senses and emotions but it could not let me forget the real flesh and bone connection between this female lineage. I too belong to a female lineage. This is my point of vision. If we come from an infinite number of children then my memories are never lonely ones, they come from a source other than myself.

How often are the images you conjure up not your own and yet you live through them as if they were. A recurring image that asks for its story and although you may have even heard its story, it is not your story to tell. So, why is it in your head? Why do you try so hard to imagine every detail and not just the details but the feelings that went with it.

The over-flowing sugar in the candy factory. Sweet, sticky sugar. It was for this same sugar, she thought, those souls in India starved. Why not package this "waste" and send it home. It made her cry. It made her cry to have to work in a factory at night in this strange new land, with its foreign tongue and offensive ways.

Was it all over the sticky ground she walked on? How did she reconcile herself to this waste? Her small feet in their black loafers getting stuck to the floor every night as she walked across the conveyor belt. She cried a lot, she told us, and only worked in that place for a month. Did she cry in the early morning rays on her way home or after she had packed a lunch for her husband who was just out the door to his job? Did she even wait that long or was she crying as the gumballs blurred in front of her eyes. She had to separate the well-formed gumballs from the broken ones before they were packaged. Her gloved hands must have worked deftly as her bright gold bangles jingled. I have never seen my mother's arms without at least a pair of gold bracelets against that brown skin. "A married woman should never have her arms bare," Ma always says. Her earlier bracelets were made of gold but were as strong as steel. They were never bent, always perfectly round. All those powerful machines she worked at to provide for her children never could bend her musical bangles out of shape. When my brothers were older and had established their shared family business, one of the things they wanted for my mother, besides early retirement, was to buy her new gold bracelets. My mother bought those bracelets on her first trip home ten years after she had first come to Canada. As beautiful as they are, they are softer and bend easier.

I was my mother's youngest daughter. A three-year-old who was waiting to keep her up all day after a hard and frightening night's work. For a woman to be out so late was hard for her to accept. She and my aunt worked the night shift but were promised the first day shift available. Even now, she smiles when she tells us how hard it was for her to stay awake. During the day, she slept with one eye open to watch over me. She was always so tired from work she would feel nauseous all day. Knowing I was making my mother sick to her stomach would have seemed like retribution to me back then.

I am lying in front of the six storey building, looking up at the third floor. We are living in a two bedroom apartment that will soon be filled with six kids but right now she is all mine. The others are still back home. I am lying on the cool grass crying. My mother is yelling from the kitchen window for me to come home, it is dark and I have been playing all day. I demand she come down and pick me up like all the other mothers have done with all my friends who are now long gone home. She laughs and tells me she is too busy cooking and that I should be her Rani, Little Queen, and come up by myself. I keep crying and refuse. She laughs, "Aja, aja. Soon the tears from your eyes will run into your ears and you won't be able to hear me any more, Archana! Come, come quick!" Fear stiffens my limbs. I am alarmed at the all-knowing power of this omnipotent witch. But I don't budge. I kick and whine, feeling the tears run cold into my warm ears. Not to hear her voice? At the time I wasn't too concerned about it. I was bellowing out my own wailing voice. Her laugh. The terror of not hearing her laugh, her sometimes cruel, taunting laugh.

Was it the sugar that made her nauseated or was it putting up with my ranting and raving? It's the sugar I have always tried to imagine. How did it spill out? I only remember enjoying all the gumballs I miraculously received. I would wake while my mother tried to sleep to find my treasures dropped on the kitchen counter. Once I found the bag of goodies, I would quickly shove my mouth full with all the candy my grubby little hands could hold. Was it in heaps of bags just pouring out as my mother walked in every night?

She had to wear pants to work — my mother. And an Indian woman, she believed, always looks most attractive in a sari. A sari — the drape that it has been called — flows and smoothes over all those parts of the body that some young women today might wish to hide. It soothes and protects our body, she said, that is otherwise so vulnerable to outside scrutiny. Her legs, thighs and chest were always covered, her milky white arms always bare and her soft tummy always ready to have a tired little head lie on it. She wasn't used to constraining polyester in between her legs. Her pants and blouse held in a stomach that had proudly borne six children. Even today my mother wears a sari more often than not. She is most comfortable in her petticoat, short-sleeved cotton top and her loosely wrapped chiffon while she cooks, cleans, naps or goes for a walk.

Growing up in Canada, I always wanted my mother to wear what everyone else's mother wore. I didn't care how uncomfortable she might feel or how ill-fitted she looked, even to me. On a hot summer day I too like to wear long flowing skirts that sway and swirl at the top of my ankles. I love the feel of a warm breeze hugging my legs and whirling up my thighs. My mother has hairless, fair legs that have seldom worshipped the sun but I am sure the wind gods have paid her their respects too. And as I recently discovered, you do not have to wear panties under a long sari or skirt! She follows me everywhere I go.

My mother's hands are not the soft hands of a loving mother. Her hands travelling over my forehead are not welcome. They hurt, they are rough and torn. Her fingertips look like hard, broken crusts of the earth. Her feet, the ones I rub over and over again with oils, are as hard as the ground she walks on. I feel robbed — robbed of a vision I have of what a mother is supposed to be. I have never seen my mother's face without the tiny creases around her eyes and mouth. I have always known her thin greying hair. Today she says I dye her hair best of all my sisters, of course I do, I have a vested interest. As I look at the old, framed photograph my sister has I say out loud, "What a beautiful woman," thinking it must be my brother-in-law's mother. The woman in the picture has paper-smooth skin, with little curls at her temples while the rest of her black hair is a long thick braid. An old black-and-white photograph that has turned a shade of earthy brown. What a stylish woman! I raise my hands up to my own temples following my hairline up to find those same baby curls.

And then there were my mother's earlobes. They always had a pair of large gold hoops in them. Not the yellow gold that my pretty blond kindergarten teacher wore, hers were a deep gold, almost orange. It was those elongated slits in her ears, rather than the usual hole, that I was at once curious about and repelled by. "In the old days," Ma tells me "we just put potatoes behind our ears and jabbed a needle through." She laughs and my upper lip curls. How barbaric!

It is my eighth birthday and my aunt is taking me to get my ears pierced. Why is Meenu, her daughter, coming along — it isn't her birthday? I thought we would arrive at a clinic of some sort where they dealt with this sort of procedure. Instead, we stop at a little ladies' clothing boutique. It isn't a woman in white that is about to pierce my tender lobes but rather a dark, short man who hasn't bothered to shave, let alone probably wash his hands in the morning. He lays the gun on the counter and to my dismay I realize how he's going to use it — like a hole punch! He is going to punch holes out of my flesh! Never mind, he at least has some alcohol rubs. He then takes out a felt pen from under his counter, to my horror licks the tip, and proceeds to mark my flesh. Stoically, I take that big gun in — it is cold, metallic and loud. He does the same to my second ear, only this earring hangs lower than the first one. This man has not marked my earlobes evenly! He insists that I have moved but I hadn't.

During this whole time my younger cousin has become quite pale — transforming into a mouse-like creature watching from behind two very large, bulging eyes. My aunt witnesses this metamorphic talent of her daughter's at the same time.

She lifts her eyebrows in surprise but then quickly turns the corners of her mouth down. Now, my cousin has to choose between the gunshot in her ear or the wrath of an embarrassed mother. She is brave enough to have one ear done but she then darts off the stool and scurries out of the reach of the onlooking adults. She turns around, flapping her hands as if she wants to fly right out of there, all the while shaking her head in refusal to the repeated torture to her other ear. Her lips are tightly pressed together and her eyes threaten to pop right out of her head. She really does seem as tiny as a mouse as I watch the adults running behind her without any success in her capture. They turn to me. I lie and betray my cowardly cousin. "Come on, it doesn't really hurt at all.... I mean, not the second time," I cajole and insist. Then I get tired of her whining, crying and cowering, and I reach into the rack of ladies dresses, grab her by the neck and yank her out. Since then, I have never really cared to wear earrings much.

As I grew older, Ma got hip to the changing fashions: I had to put buttons behind her ears in order for her to wear studs. "My god, mother, why are your holes so big?" She smiles and replies, "I wore real gold. No eighteen carats for me. No, not like you girls today, putting anything in your ears. Twenty-four or nothing at all!"

We laugh. My golden brown goddess laughs with me. It seems that for every story of my mother's I have a counter story — a pair of golden hoops intertwined. The mirror image in a different time and in a different place. Will my daughter have my story, mingled with my mother's and her own to tell? At twenty-three I wonder, have I honestly given an account of what happened in that shop more than fifteen years ago? Could I possibly, even if I did want to? Would it then still be worth telling? The web we weave when first we tell a lie is perhaps, for most women, the tales they spin into a fabric of comfort and warmth.

I have said that I don't wear earrings — they just don't sit right with me! At seventeen though, I did want at least one pair of small gold hoops. Hoops had come back into fashion and so had getting back to your roots. My mother had some brought over from the land of silks, gold and spices. She gave them to me for Christmas.

Holding these two special circles I ran to the bathroom to look at myself in the mirror while I put them on. To my horror, one fell down the drain. After dismantling the sink it was still not to be found. Ma just laughed at how clumsy I was as usual. I didn't find it as funny. I still have the one gold hoop and she has since mentioned getting me the other one. But I only have half of what she has given me. I have half of who she is.

LOPA BANERJEE

On Women, Asleep

How peacefully they lie,
their bodies in sleep
what they cannot be awake —
languorous
the heavy limbs curl upon
themselves
with sated sweetness.
The light limbs, spread out,
floating, free.

One tosses.
What restless thought pierces
the abandoned symmetry of her form?
She reaches out.
Her sleep-intoxicated limbs tangle with
the other's.
She stretches in silent reply.
Their bodies mingle.
I see them,
lying self to self
and wonder at their unstilled
passions.

Vermilion on Your Forehead

Ah my friend!
The vermilion on your forehead
Was not so bright
As the smile you gave me
In return to the tremulous
Question you saw in my eyes,
That day.

And when I embraced
You
You stifled the murmur
Of my arms
By looking at him
In whose life you now
Belonged ...
"That was a long time ago"
You say.

Today
The vermilion
Is redder than the crimson
Of your sari
And the clink of your
Glass bangles
Sound louder than your voice ...
Somewhere along,
There is a meaning.
Will you ever learn to figure
It out?
Will I?

Ramabai Espinet

Cane in Arrow

A DOG WAS RUNNING along the highway at the side. The day was hot, a hot dry Sunday afternoon, and she was in panic. She ran steadily at the side, dugs loose and flapping, tongue hanging and dry, skin slack. She was a short brown dog.

Around her, the cane fields stretched for miles, green and limitless, their silver arrows shooting for the sky. She belonged to no one; she was going nowhere. The cars sped by going east; she was headed west. I read the panic in that dog's eyes.

She had that sense of being alive common, I believe, to all living things — have mercy on us, mercy — caught in the dread game we call life. Death ran up and down the highway, stalking the little bitch, or maybe just indifferently cutting her down. Death didn't really care. Neither did she.

When I passed back later, evening was shifting through the canes, and there was a restlessness in the air. The light was that marvelous tropical amber that we get in the early months of the year, the frogs were settling down for the evening, the wind was cool. There was a small brown dead dog in a quiet heap at the side of the road. It could have been her. I don't know.

Once (and acting upon a dare) I attempted to seduce Death. He fell for it and held me in his arms, loved, stroked and comforted me, and all the while he planned how to take me with him into his velvet kingdom. He took me away from everything, no questions asked. I renounced the world, all other flesh, and what remained of my life. I lived safely for a time in his dark kingdom.

When I felt pain it was all of a piece, the world's pain and my own, stretching myself through and across boundaries I could not have even known existed. You might have been seduced too. Don't doubt it, you're the same, the same.

I lived with Death and loved him. It was the breaking of another barrier. It was only when I crashed on the other side that I knew that this had been the most insurmountable one yet. In that time I gathered energy by asking questions and leaving questions on my mind. I found that there are no answers to many questions. Crashing through I knew that I had crossed. I had crossed; I had crossed something.

I dreamt of a man last night. Just an acquaintance — but no, that's a lie. Someone a little closer than that and not part of my life at all. He was bewildered; he walked or rather flapped about a large flat terrain, as unmarked and guideless as a concrete carpark. He seemed to be looking around for some kind of signal from a guide who was not yet a part of the dream-frame, but no cue came and he was forced to meander, flapping helplessly, until he erased himself.

The dream light grew later and it was evening when he wandered in again. Evidently he had been exposed to some kind of experience — a devastating experience.

Time is important here, time, and there's no time left.

Time was designated by a distribution of light on the wide

expanse of undifferentiated land surface. The earlier time was morning — clear and luminous. The evening was characterized by red, urgent and desperate, ticking in short rapid breaths.

He moved uncertainly on the flat concrete as the surface changed and he began to ascend a small hill. As he rose to the top his full form came into view and stabbed me to the heart with all its unstated implications. His shirt still flapped around his form, ill-fitting as usual, too long and badly curved, but this could not conceal the fact that he had lost his pants and that he now wore a pair of cheap, flimsy, whitish drawers completely wrecked on the behind. The crotch seams had separated from each other and hung loosely down. There was only a tiny suggestion of blood and wet, wet, human wreckage. And worst of all was the helpless, half-apologetic look on his face.

There must be a breaking point in every life — animal, vegetable or mineral — after which nothing is of consequence any more and acquiescence sets in. It is impossible to establish a schedule for calculating exactly when this giving up takes root and I have heard people theorize about its origins in the womb. Every living thing must have an internal code for determining the exact moment when stress becomes insupportable and extinction the only release.

The death of a small brown dog is not inconsequential. The man I once knew holds on to life, destroyed, gathering up his questions into fresh apologies or acts of non-recognition. The frogs settle down for the evening, the cane is in arrow on the horizon, the beautiful light shifts and changes. I could die of grief.

A Piece of Indian Junk

Radha waiting for Krishna ...
Will he come?
Through thickets of time
Hidden in forests
She has waited
For three hundred years

Outside a tomb in Chandigarh
A woman remembers:
He gave me a necklace
— A *chandahar* —
Wear this
I shall know you
Even after three hundred
Years

She stands on a hill
Watches
Outside a tomb in Chandigarh
Watches
His face impetuous
His hair, dangerous eyes
Flashing hillward
Watches
As they kill him
She hears
Nothing

The *chandahar* swings
Through three centuries

Its crescents map
Newer histories
Isolate geographies
Indian, Antillean, strange
Time curves into
Journeys far from
Home

Travelling through airports
Passports, tickets
— *Les baggages de deplacements* —
A woman
Finds a necklace
She thinks:
Old Indian work,
On an impulse
She buys it
Later, a friend
With a jeweller's eye
Turns it over:
"A piece of Indian junk
Not worth five dollars
Throw it out"

Then on New Year's Eve
Dressed to kill
She
Wears the thing
Times Square madness
Friends, wine
A homeless man
The first to say
Happy New Year

A street musician playing
Auld Lang Syne
That first morning
On the streets of New York

Four o'clock in the morning
She walks into
A room full of strangers
A man crosses the floor
Asks her to dance
Their brown hands touch
For no reason they quarrel
She walks away
And menacingly he follows
Into the kitchen

Intimidation;
His style
No boundaries
Intimidation
Was it some kind of joke?

When did she start
To talk to him?
When realize
She wants to talk
To him
Without stopping

"Why did you cross the room?"
(Long afterwards)
"Because of this,"
Touching the piece
Of Indian junk

She wants nothing more
Than to continue
Talking to him
Talking ...

Days later
The conversation still going
In her head
She manages a telephone call
He cries out,
"Hey, it's you!
I haven't seen you
For three hundred years...."

The telephone line crackles
A thousand chasms away
She touches the piece
Of old
Indian
Junk
And listens to
His voice.

Dare to Bare

AH FIND THIS THING about breasts full of contradiction, yes.

Women say they challenging the indecency laws by taking off they shirt. Men say they not indecent when they take off they own shirt. But they say that women indecent and they should arrest them when they do the same thing, and doh mind that, they go push and shove and run up with camera and camcorder and all kinda thing to see the women and them "in a state of indecency."

Is a funny world for true when on a hot day, or at the beach, any man could yawn and stretch and take off he shirt. Yuh think a woman could do the same? Well think again.

In the demonstration in Waterloo over the weekend, I see a young woman protesting with she breasts taped down solid with black tape and CENSORED scrawl all over it. That is a symbol for repression mother in truth!

So wha' wrong with breasts? A breast is a natural, functional organ. Is the receptacle of mother's milk. Is the best source of sustenance for a newborn infant. Is a moral, wholesome thing. Why all the shame and scandal associated with this particular body part?

Part a the problem is really because de people in charge, de world of consumerism and advertising and dem tings, dey need to mystify, package, sell and control the female body. So woman cleavage now convert into a kinda time-share.

Yuh could use cleavage to sell everything from motor-car to pretzel these days and people go buy. It just go to show how much power and control a woman body could have if she decide to really use it in the skin trade.

So when woman decide that all a de whole power structure doh own she breasts but that is she and she alone who go decide when she dare to bare, or when she choose to cover up, or when and where she go breast-feed she baby, then de whole power structure does start to shiver and shake and get really frighten.

They feel that it go be de end of the world as they know it. And yuh know something? Don't think is only a feeling. Is de God truth, yuh hear me?

Because de day that all kinda woman get up and say listen man, is my body and you can't tell me how to jam it into dis or dat or de other shape, and if mih breasts stand up straight or fall below me waist is mine, and who tell you God put me here just to be a object of beauty for you eh? Man, I just living mih life so leh me pass, yuh hear. De day all kinda woman get up and say that, well, is all fall down.

When that day come, all kinda vice and peep-show go fall flat on they face just so. Who go want to pay to siddown in some dark lil tavern in the middle of the day, drinking beer and watching TV while some poor lady, struggling to support two/three fatherless chirren, have to take off she bodice and bring dey beer just to get a few dollars?

All that kinda thing go be dead when people see breast as normal and natural. Buh human beings so perverse. They so like scandal and bacchanal it ain't funny. From the time God pelt we outa de Garden of Eden we dey chasing down forbidden fruit. De day breast get normal and natural, ten to one they go dress up a arm or a leg and turn it into some other kinda fetish. It look like we can't help it. That is how we stop.

And yuh know why? Because it have a dream of power and control. Everybody have de dream, that ain't no secret. Is just that de power and control right now in the hands of the man and dem. And they ain't go give up power and control so easy.

Yuh want to know why breasts have to keep lock up? Not because every man in town go turn rapist when he see the occasional pair of boobs sauntering casually by. Not because a that. Is because woman own body is not they own. Man must regulate it, say when to take off clothes, and how much, where to nurse your baby and so on.

Man have a stake in breast-commerce, yuh hear. They done seize woman breast and then go and sell it to other man in strip joint, in advertising, "cheesecake" and ting. Is a kinda exchange they know bout. Man don't like woman to give away she body for free. She must value sheself. That mean she must sell sheself under the tradegrounds them set up already.

That is why they really run to see with camcorder and camera and ting. To catch a "piece" of the action. And when they see a set a women marching with they shirt on, and some man without shirt marching with them, they start to bawl, "Bare your breasts!" One righteous fella even say, "Buh allyuh is something else yes. Allyuh ain't even live up to allyuh convictions!"

As far as I could see de only conviction in he head was the conviction to see a "free-show." How much more miles to cross, Mudda?

Dare to bare? Yeah! is a ordinary natural ting. Is a ordinary, NORMAL part a we body. What is indecent about breasts?

This article is written in the Caribbean Creole English common to Trinidad, with snatches of Jamaican and Guyanese Creoles interspersed.

KISHWAR NAHEED

Speech No. 27

My voice is the voice of the town.
My voice is the voice of my generation.
My voice will echo through generation after generation.
What makes you call my speech madness!
Why do you presume to pronounce
The advancing tempest to be an illusion?

I am not a messenger.
I am just looking carefully at today.
The stench of your animal-smell
Spreads in the shape of lust for money.
You recline in the back seat of your limousine
So that the harsh sun of poverty
May not scorch your plastic face.

You remember your speeches by their numbers.
Speech number 10, to rouse poor,
Speech number 15, to awaken awareness in women,
Speech number 27, to advise writers and thinkers.

Voices, voices, voices
What is clamour?
The noise of shapeless voices,
Or the surge of incoherent speeches?
Stones are rolling,
If you throw stones in the desert
You see them sink in the sand
Without even a whisper,
But my voice is my stone;
It is lightning which flashes first
And then thunders.
Putting your hands over your ears
Does not stop the storms coming.

Those who deliver speeches about the weather
By reading about it:
When will they come
To see drains flooding the streets?
Planting the sapling of revolution.

You can buy a lot of red dye for two *annas*,
But scarves coloured in the dye of two *annas*,
Cannot reflect the colour of blood.
When even I know all this
How come you don't know it!
I speak the truth.
I am not a messenger.
I am just looking carefully at today.

First Priority of Third-Class Citizens

We need to speak
Even with our mouths on the ground.
My innocence pleads,
Mouth on the ground,
That fear is laid
On all pathways of life
At the command of the city's ruler.
Not many who speak
Are left in town.
We really should cut off their heads
And treasure them as souvenirs.
Such people will not be seen again.
I swear by god
That even when my eyes become blisters,
I will still cry,
Since cries grow in my fields.
The stagnant quiet in my courtyards
Robs my children of their laughter.

My office boy refuses the uniform,
The symbol of third-class citizens.
The matter is beyond uniforms and symbols.
Whether the symbol
Of the severed tail of the lizard
Or the meaning of the stench of blood —
All are the names of fear.
We are exiles in our city.
We soulless living beings,
Are devoid of even the will to speak.

Self-Reckoning

When the last crow of the last cock sounds,
When the morning star announces
The end of the last night;
And when the sun of the last day
Brings the message of blood-spitting morning,
I will lift my head from the pillow
And take account of my last breaths.

After the last politician has killed
The last man;
After the last child has died
Searching for the last grain of rice;
After the last drop of blood is spent
In defence of the motherland;
After the last word of prayer is spent;
After the last bullet pierces the chest,
I will lift my head from the pillow
And take account of my last breaths.

When the last child suckles in vain
The breasts of the last corpse;
When the orphan child calls his mother
To curse the rulers;
When man sets foot for the last time
On the last moon,
I will lift my head from the pillow
And take account of my last breaths.

When the last kiss records life;
When the generation learns to bear fear

As pleasure;
And even space
Is a picture of hypocrisy,
I will lift my head from the pillow
And take account of my last breaths.

The Rain within Myself

To you, I was a window.
You opened me
And enjoyed the scene as you pleased,
And inhaled the breeze and colours.
To seek shelter from the storm,
You closed the shutter
And I became a robe
Snugly wrapped around you.

To you, I was a tunnel
In which you could shelter when you wished
And could conceal me, too.
To keep your footprints from sight,
You walked in me for life.

To you, I was a dream;
I was water;
I was sand;
I was reality on command;
And like indigestion's after-taste,
Forgotten.

When you talk in your dreams,
I have to listen lying awake.
But no dream listens
To my wakeful words.

After Thought

The agony of living more than fifty years
Is not like the agony of living less than fifty years.
Had the change occurred
Only in my hair, face and body,
Or my complexion and form,
I wouldn't have felt it.
But it seems
That the faces of others
And their eyes embedded in them
Have changed in the way
That didn't seem possible
Fifty years ago.
Fifty years ago.
It was also unlikely
That sons and daughters,
Waiting to collect
Their parents' insurance pension,
Couldn't stand their parents any longer.
Or that sons, compelled by the desire to fly high,
Would have to keep their parents
In the servants' quarters;
Or that in the madness of desire,
The confused sons and daughters

Would have to seek help of
Local witch doctors
To cut short their parents' lives.
In those countries
Where there are no old folks' homes
Growing old should not be allowed.
In the long string of unjust laws,
Pass another such law,
Fifty years!
Let this be the limit of one's life.

TRANSLATED BY BAIDAR BAKHT,
LESLIE LAVIGNE AND DEREK M. COHEN

DAMAYANTHI FERNANDO

Roses for My Dead Friend

THE TRAIN SLOGGED ON along the coastal track in the gathering darkness. Several unscheduled stops were made to check the tracks for bombs and land mines. I sat by the window in an empty disinfected compartment, weighed down by depression and fear. Although the medical school was closed down, my parents had persuaded me to remain in Colombo as my home town was engulfed in civil strife. In Colombo, I was helping my uncle at his office. It took as long as two years for me and my parents to realize that emergency is a matter of everyday life. The university still remained closed. At the end of two years, however, I decided to go home.

The train reached Matara, my home town, around eight at night. It was 1989. The usually busy station was deserted. The single fluorescent bulb cast an eerie glow on its surroundings. A wiry little man dressed in a porter's uniform informed me that the curfew was in force, as usual.

"A curfew?" I said, blankly.

"The Nationalists have imposed it," he said, and scurried off like a frightened rabbit.

There were no vehicles in the dark, ill-lit street. Even the buggy carts which transferred the less affluent were not parked outside the station. Shops were closed and army soldiers carrying automatic rifles stood stiff and motionless.

I walked along the main road and turned towards a narrow gravel path to take a short-cut home. Fear gripped me as I became aware of the danger in the situation. I began to run as fast as I could. Suddenly, two figures emerging from the darkness grabbed me.

"You are breaking the law," said one of them, shaking me violently by the shoulders as the other flashed a torch in my face. I saw two boys, both armed with rifles, but neither of them could have been more than fifteen or sixteen years old. I managed to stammer an explanation that seemed to satisfy them, for they offered to escort me home. We walked in silence for some time.

"Why are the streets and houses in darkness?" I asked, to avoid tension and fear.

"We have forbidden them to light lamps or use electricity for three days," answered the taller one, with a touch of pride and authority in his voice.

Suddenly, a motor vehicle approached us without its headlights on. Went past, stopped, a few feet ahead. With lightning speed my companions pulled me to an overgrown hedge. Four men jumped off the vehicle, a jeep; one of them carried a torch. They went to a small house by the street, kicked the door open, went in and dragged a man out. We heard loud accusations and protests of innocence. I could only see dimly in the obscure light but I recognized Ranjith's voice.

"I know that man," I told my companions.

They slapped me to silence.

The men assaulted Ranjith, our servant, with fierce brutality. His agonized screams rent the air. Mercifully, the man with the torch shot him. They tied his body up to a large tree by the roadside and fled.

None of us spoke until we reached my house.

"Thank you for the great kindness," I said, but my companions did not speak and disappeared swiftly into the darkness.

I went around the back of the house and tapped at the kitchen window. Nervous strain and physical exhaustion overwhelmed me. I fell into my mother's arms and sobbed hysterically.

"They killed Ranjith, they shot him," I said, crying.

"Thank god you are safe." Mother wiped my face with the edge of her cotton sari.

"You exposed yourself to grave danger," my father said with disapproval.

"Why do you think they killed Ranjith, Mother?"

"They say he was a terrorist, a member of the Nationalist revolutionaries."

"Nonsense, the poor fellow had no political convictions of any kind," contradicted my father.

"Then who could have killed him, Papa?" I blinked tearfully.

"It could be the army, the revolutionaries, or any one of the paramilitary groups; it is difficult to say."

"Two days ago he was brutally assaulted by the army for pasting anti-government posters," said mother.

"Ranjith told me he was forced to do it by the Nationalist revolutionaries," interjected our cook.

"We don't know what to think any more," said mother, handing me a cup of hot tea.

Later in bed I kept thinking of Ranjith for a long time. My memory took me years back in my life, when I was a child:

My mother had a passion for roses. She did not permit any other flower in her garden. My earliest conversations with her were on the subject of roses. Once, my mother caught me in the act of picking a large pink rose; she was furious.

"If you pick any of my roses, you are going to hurt yourself," she warned me, pressing both my arms against the thorny twigs.

I was terrified.

On my fourth birthday, as I walked among rose bushes a bright idea crossed my creative mind. With a plastic spade I made little mounds of sand around the front porch of our house. Then I began to pick roses. It was far more difficult than I had anticipated. Most of the roses refused to be pinched and clung stubbornly to the branches, maimed and bruised after grappling bravely with me. Undeterred, I worked on till I had a rose stuck on each mound of sand.

Mother was busy in the kitchen applying icing on my birthday cake.

"Come, Mother, I have something to show you," I said, pulling her by the arm.

I made her close her eyes and guided her to the front porch. Mother opened her eyes slowly, surveyed my rose garden, then hers. Contrary to my expectations, her face turned purple with rage.

"Disobedient rascal," she screamed, striking with her open palms.

I cried aloud more out of shock than pain. Mother had never hit me before.

Ranjith, our servant, came to my rescue. He brushed away my tears and carried me to the river bank at the back of our house.

"A posy for the pretty princess," he said with an exaggerated bow, handing me a bunch of wild flowers.

"Thank you, Ranjith," I laughed, kissing him. "They are much prettier than Mother's roses."

The following year I was sent to a boarding school in Colombo, a long way from home.

Ranjith's honest face floated before me in the darkness till I fell asleep.

I rose early the following morning and walked to the spot where Ranjith's body stood tied against the rain tree. His body was covered with large red ants; thousands of them were busy supping on dry caked blood splattered all over the body.

Two police officers arrived soon after. They untied the body while eyeing me suspiciously. They dumped his body on top of the pile of corpses in a pickup and drove away.

That evening my father took the body to Ranjith's home, a daub-and-wattle hut.

"I got permission to hand over the body for burial," said my father to Ranjith's distraught wife. "It must be done as soon as possible," he added.

"Thank you sir, you've been very helpful." She touched my father's feet and wept bitterly.

A man from the Rodia caste took Ranjith's body to the back of the house and prepared it for burial. In the crude wooden coffin, he looked so different. Bereft of his gentle spirit, his body was an empty shell. My mother consoled the bereaved while our cook served refreshments in her efficient unobtrusive way.

I took Ranjith's little girl to the river bank and played with her. She was too young to understand or grieve her father's death. The little girl pointed out an ugly monitor. It moved with a sinister sensuality towards the bushes and dragged out the bullet-ridden body of a young girl. The enormous lizard mounted the body and tore off the left breast and started to eat it.

That could have been me.

Fate had been kind to me.

That night I sat with my parents outside Ranjith's house. A few friends and neighbours stood in scattered groups talking softly in muffled voices. The air was thick with the pungent odour emitted from the clay pots containing herbs, *margosa* oil and red hot coals. The fumes drowned the unpleasant odour and acted as a disinfectant. Ranjith's house was illuminated by a single petromax lamp, my wedding present to him.

Suddenly, several masked figures emerged from the surrounding darkness and strode into the house. We followed them, frightened and bewildered. Gathered around the coffin, the masked men conjured a weird spectacle. With no warning, one man stepped forward, spat on the corpse, and shot at the petromax lamp. It crashed down on the coffin and started a fire. The intruders disappeared with speed. Confusion, followed by stampeding panic, engulfed us all. Ranjith's wife embraced the burning corpse; soon her clothes and hair were on fire. Smoke blurred my vision, I felt my mother pulling me towards the exit. People were trying to get out screaming in terror.

Some time later, my father and a few neighbours brought Ranjith's wife and daughter into our house. They were badly burned. There was very little we could do by way of first aid. The hospitals were closed by the Nationalists and the doctors forbidden to treat the sick. After much deliberation my parents took the injured to a family friend who was a doctor.

I woke to the sounds of dogs howling, barking and fighting among themselves. The sound came from the direction of Ranjith's house. I stepped out into the cool morning breeze and started to walk briskly towards the burned-down house. The cook and my old *ayah* followed me bidding me to come back and threatening me with the dire consequences of my parents' wrath. From a distance I could see dogs tearing off flesh from Ranjith's partly charred naked body. The old *ayah* shielded my eyes with her palms.

I cried till there were no more tears left in me.

"We must bury the body," I said after a while.

The cook went back and returned with a male servant. He dug a shallow grave a little distance away while the two women covered what was left of the body with an old table-cloth.

After the burial, I went to my mother's rose garden; the roses were fresh and beautiful as ever. I gathered an armful, walked back to Ranjith's grave and stuck each rose separately on the mound of soft earth.

RENUKA SOOKNANAN

Desert Storm

We sit and watch
Mother and child
caught
in a
Desert of Storm.

the soldiers in
Green and
Black

Green and Black:
Dressed in Green
they are Black.
My brothers and
Sisters
caught
in a
desert of storm.

Heroine

It is in understanding
the depths of this struggle,
to approach the crossroads
and not know the boundaries
because for us there are none.
It is to caress a flickering lamp
glowing a beautiful hope
because darkness is sure to follow.
In this struggle,
we,
I understand
my heroine
is today, was yesterday
will be tomorrow.
Marching somewhere
chanting loudly
writing feverishly
sleeping seldomly
between resisting and battle
never knowing
what strength is needed
to rise out of bed
to congregate amongst the hungry masses
fighting for the revolution.
My heroine is someone
I don't know.

Can I Be Trini?

Walking the street
toting the market basket
Nanny on my other side.

Stop, find a seat.

I know she thinking
she eyes glazed, eyebrows knotted.
She hair combed to a
bun in the air supporting she
white and silver *orhni*.
The ingredients are here
staring me down, as Nanny's gold
jingles cling, clang.

"Hum! This taxi driver dotish, eh?"
"Take it easy, Nan."
Cling, clang:
"Driver drop we out by Mosaih Hardware."

"Yes, Nanny, yuh gran'daughter nice to bad."
"Shut yuh ass," cheupsing under her breath.

Adjusting once again she *orhni* crossing the street.
Toting the basket, cautious
not to let its contents go astray.
Nan going to cook
everybody's favourite

fresh *bhaji*

cut from the drain pipe
carrots bought
from a little boy in Chaguanas market
the other, more true addition
caught earlier that morning.

I can't believe it
standing by the fireside
watching
each ingredient melting
one into the other
slowly
the consistency growing
thicker but still
slowly.

Sitting at the table
staring at the melted pot
dished into even portions.
Wondering, how to tell Nan.
"Beti, wha'pen, ya na hungry?"
Sunday.
Everyone
all over Trinidad
enjoying the same
green,
blended consistency.

How can I not like *calaloo*?
Can I be Trini?

LASANDA KURUKULASURIYA

Brown & White

White woman smiles behind glass pane
handing out forms.
Brown woman in her gaudy sari
smiles back automatically
shows all thirty-two
on the slightest provocation
as she is wont to do.
White woman's face freezes
suddenly, her smile turns queer.
Doesn't this foolish woman know that we
may condescend to smile, but we
may not be too familiar?

Subway

Sitting in the subway car
What moves? the station or the train?

So many tons of steel
Running in to the tunnel
Time is running out

In the subway
Out the street
Continual scuffle of hurrying feet
Catching up with reality
Time passes

MALIKA JAYASINGHE

A Private Affair

I HAD BEEN ABOUT TWELVE years of age when the woman came to live in our house. A fair creature of about twenty with a honey tan and coal black hair, she had been brought in to assist my mother with the household chores.

Later, much later, I realized that her face had had strength and beauty and that her eyes, yes, her eyes were what one would have noticed most for they could become hard or warm, depending on whom she had been looking at.

I had hardly paid any attention to her till I saw her walk surreptitiously into my father's room when all the others were locked in sleep. It had been a cold and windy day. Disturbed by the loud chirping of some night birds and unable to sleep, I paced the floor around midnight. The half-open window of my father's room offered a fine view of everything that happened inside it.

There had been times before this when I had caught my father and the woman looking at each other in a strange way, oblivious of all else. Once, on a day we had celebrated a family anniversary, I had seen my father standing aside and gazing at her with a strange kind of fascination. She in turn had smiled coyly and then they had simply kept on staring at each other till the woman, seeing me, had blushed and turned her gaze to the cold hard floor.

My father, a compact man with a Van Dyke beard, had always had an air of cloudless serenity. I had believed it had been the retreat of a man who tried to get away from a mean little world. Later, I realized that his hypocritical manners were as fake as my mother's jewellery: thinly plated with the glitter of gold and false propriety.

I had been around sixteen years when I began to understand the full meaning of those nocturnal visits and clandestine meetings. An appalling thought! I had willed myself not to think about it yet I felt physically sick whenever such thoughts surfaced.

I remember one incident very vividly. It was Sinhala New Year's day and I was awakened by the stir and bustle of this special occasion. There were the sounds of exploding crackers, the throbbing of *rabanas* and the constant incantations of elders. Then the partaking of the "new" meal and the customary exchange of money at the prescribed time. After the transactions between the family members had been completed, my father had walked up to the woman, who had stood aside all the time, and dropped a betel-wrapped wad of money onto her palm. Had their hands touched, lingered a trifle longer than was necessary? I thought I saw their eyes locked for a while before they began to move away from each other.

Had my mother noticed it? Had she ever noticed any of the untoward happenings that were taking place under her own roof? Even if she had, I think there was little she could have done about it. What had left my mother weaponless was the fact that my father had behaved with dignity and decorum when the woman was not around. All one really saw was a deep and inner change within him, a kind of darkening of his usual sunny self.

Yet, that night, I heard my mother's voice raised high in anger. So she had noticed the little game that had been played that evening.

"I don't want her to stay here a minute longer. I will order her out of the house in the morning." Her voice had trembled with emotion.

"No. The woman will stay. You have no right to interfere with anything or anyone in MY house," my father had roared.

A profound silence followed.

It must have been a galling situation for my mother, yet a mood of peace had prevailed for some time. Maybe they had entered into a quiet rapprochement. But I had sensed an uneasiness, a kind of lingering resentment between them.

Soon, the short leash on which my mother was trying to hold back her anger snapped under days of strain. I had had to close my ears to the constant fights and open arguments of those stormy broken days. The marriage, it seemed then, had been severely rent.

Things came to a head the day she found the beautiful gold pocket watch in the woman's room. It had been in the family for four generations and my father had been particularly attached to it. It was an exquisite watch. The enamel lid encircled by pearls showed Cupid disarmed by Venus; the scalloped edge of the watch had been painted with bouquets and musical instruments, and a gold dial showed the time.

Once, attracted by its beauty, I had taken it in my hand, prised open the lid and was watching its magical intricacies when my father had snatched it from me and reprimanded me severely for it. Perhaps the woman had not been aware that in receiving this family heirloom she had picked up a loaded gun.

I had found my mother pacing the floor inside her room that day and my father staring fixedly out of the window. I had stopped in my tracks as I heard my mother shout, "You gave it to her, didn't you?" Her rage had seemed uncontrollable.

A few seconds of thunderous silence and then my father exploded.

"Yes, so what about it?" His voice rose and struck her like a slap, because by saying that, my father had admitted the truth — that he was having an affair with the woman.

My mother remained silent for a long time. It must have taken time for her to absorb the shock. When she finally spoke, her voice was rough with a fierce feeling and her eyes momentarily flashed with fire.

"It is despicable, this thing you are doing behind my back." Beneath her sharp words there still seemed a shade of doubt.

For a moment, it seemed, he nodded his head as if in agreement, pondering maybe on the hidden truth of my mother's words.

All that time we stood where we were, my mother and I, grasping at straws, groping for some reassurance from my father, searching for a shred of decency that might have lain hidden behind that icy facade.

Suddenly his face changed. There was naked hostility in his eyes and a tightness in his jaw, making his tone dangerous as he spoke.

"You have no right to question me about what I choose to do with MY life. Remember, I can do what I please. Never, never question me again."

I saw my mother wince. The verbal knife had plunged deep.

A kind of uncontrollable anger had welled up within me. I

had been twenty years of age then and felt that I had to intervene, protect my mother from my father's flagrant infidelity. There was no excuse for his outrageous behaviour. I moved up to him.

"Father, I think you are being grossly unfair by my mother."

I went to her and put my arms around her comfortingly. After what had seemed an age I felt my mother quietly release herself from my grasp, then turn to my father.

"What do you want me to do? Stand by and watch this fiasco?"

A cold panic had invaded my heart. Before my father could even absorb the words, I said, "I think you should leave him, mother. After all, no woman should endure this kind of humiliation."

The words struck my father like a thunderclap. I saw his head move back instinctively, as if a sudden blow had landed on top of it.

"Yes," I heard my mother say, nodding her head. "I can't take this any more. I am leaving you."

She had spoken softly and without emotion. The game had come alive, the drama turning into a kind of ghastly end.

I still remember my father's whitened face as he turned towards my mother and asked, "You don't mean it?" Then something like a red fire had flared briefly in his eyes. His face twitched. Remorse? Worry? Maybe he was making mental calculations about winning. About losing!

He stood silently for a long time. There hadn't been the thunder we had expected; no noise, no raving, no ranting. He merely turned on his heels and walked out of the room.

Yes, my mother did leave the house a couple of days later. It was a dark day, the sky bleak, the winds brisk. She left me too — to a terrible loneliness and an eerie silence that enveloped me and our home from then on.

Time rolls back and the pictures in my mind come alive even though they are almost twenty years old. The memories of that awful time still remain. I know now what my father would have once known — the brush of panic, the feel of icy air in every pore, the dreaded footsteps that could lead to discovery ... and shame!

The woman who lives in our house now is as beautiful as the "other" woman who, ostensibly, had trampled on our domestic harmony many years ago. This one has the same oval face, black brooding eyes and a pale luminous skin.

She is my wife's friend. She moved in with us after her mother's death had left her homeless and without any resources.

I had barely noticed her at first but after a few years I found myself being drawn to her. Who can define the exact point at which indifference turns to interest and then to passion.

My wife's voice cuts across my brain like a knife.

"I always thought of you as a man of honour — no lies, no deceit, no cheating. You have changed, haven't you?" Her voice emerges in a short sharp rap — like an indictment.

I take it from her without flinching. Silently we stand inside the room listening to the faint coo of doves in their high cove above while the sky outside darkens like a bruise.

She is looking at me as if she is expecting me to say something. A faint mocking smile twists one corner of her mouth as she watches me transcribe my words.

"A man cannot lead a damned monk's life all the time, can he?"

A narrowing of eyelids, the flutter of brows. It is an atmospheric thing — like a sharp drop in a barometer. And there is the promise of thunder!

"You are doing a despicable thing."

Is it my mother's voice that I hear? It is the same sonorous voice with its rolled "r"s and clipped "t"s. My thoughts scatter into a thousand kaleidoscopic pieces. My mother's accusing voice, the hysterical outbursts ... and yes, my father's lies, his excuses. How far had that infinite mockery gone? And yet —

Yet no wife has the right to limit a man's life, tell him to do this or stop doing that.

"I'll do as I please. You can't imprison me in my own house," I hear myself say. I am my own master, I am a man who can love whom I want to love.

"But there has to be some sanctity in marriage," my wife says.

The exchange of words heats up.

My eyes stray again, first to the floor, then to the window. Across the sky white gulls zoom, their snowy wings stretched to an incredible span. Freedom! How I long for it myself.

My mind spins in a grim circle once again. How had my mother looked at the time my father was having his liaison with the other woman? Yes, I remember it now. She had been a shade untidy, a little careless in dress ... not quite what a man expected of his wife.

I look at my wife intently. Her hair dishevelled, her sari thrown carelessly over her shoulder and yes ... there are hair-like lines under her eyes.

I can speak without fear now.

"Men are different from women. That's how they are made. Every wife should understand that ... and make allowances for it. Do you hear ..."

My words get lost as my wife's voice trails behind my own.

"Don't waste your breath," I hear her say. "No need to explain. What I have been trying to tell you all this time is that I will be leaving soon."

Bated breath, the remorseless tick of a clock — a faceless frightening sound. I look around helplessly. The flat glare of the afternoon has mellowed and is now throwing shadows on the grey carpet.

A corner of my eye catches the quick embattled half turn of her head. And then I see her looking at me with a kind of vacant stare, then she turns and walks towards the door.

"Wait, let me explain," I almost shout.

She doesn't turn back.

There is a flutter of light as the door opens. I see the thin lines on her sari dancing in the sudden puff of wind as she turns the corner and disappears from sight.

RINA SINGH

A Visit to a Funeral Home

I dreamt
it was a kind of dream
at least partly
I walked into a funeral home
I'm waiting in the dimly lit hallway
I don't know what time it is
you can never tell time
in a dream
and it doesn't matter
in a funeral home, anyway
I hear steps
of the owner himself
dressed in a grey suit
a dark tie
greased hair
all prepared for a stranger's death
he greets me
with no expression
he doesn't really know if someone is already dead

or is about to die
I'm just making enquiries
I wave a newspaper clipping at him
he smiles
his well practised smile
and leads me to his office
it smells of disinfected death
he proudly shows me
the new catalogue
of coffins
tells me about
the improved services
of the cosmetician
in case of an accident
I'm interested in cremation
and I would prefer to die
peacefully
But you still need a box, lady
his silence seems to say
instead he tells me
how the popularity
of cremations
is on the rise
some people actually prefer
ashes over worms
now he wants to tell me
all about containers
all about the amazing crematorium
The whole process takes
only a few minutes
Amazing isn't it?
I live all these years
in this body

I buy it clothes
every season
I perfume it for occasions
I exercise to keep it fit
For years
I let somebody suck the hell
out of me
and you will eliminate it
in a few minutes?
I have an excuse in death
what's your hurry?
with the advertisement I have
he will make me an incredible
one day offer
If I buy my funeral today
he pays the tax
on my death
Don't tempt me
I have a weak heart
I try to joke with him
his weak smile
makes my stomach turn
Viewing me as a tough customer
in these times of recession
he extends the offer
and very generously adds
if I call back by Friday
he will throw in one free coffin
"You mean buy one get one free?"
"Exactly. But you pay your own taxes.
Government fees additional."
His turn to joke
Yes, but I need time to decide

I need to have a conference
with my family
I need an answer to why
this Government needs
to charge fees
from dead bodies
On my way out
of this dream
I'm thinking
who can I take for a drive?

Itch

You probably don't understand
the growing passions
of this lover
when she wants you
she wants you right away
she demands your fingers
she doesn't care if you are at
a cocktail party
a business meeting
a lecture
the world
can wait
but not she
the more you ignore her
the louder she gets
"Here, here," she says.
"Later," you whisper.

"Now, do it now, you bastard," she says.
You excuse yourself
behind a table
a wall even a newspaper will do
you quickly etch
your initials
on her soul
"Yes! Yes!" she groans.
It is only later
when you are alone with her
will she bitch
about the brutality
of your claws.

Pain

my grandmother could talk about it
endlessly
till one day
it got lodged permanently
in her head
and she sealed all the doors
she pulled down the shutters
of her pores
only the winds
were let loose
in her brains
she abandoned my grandfather
to the servants
her body belonged

to the silent stars
in cloudless skies
"enough is enough,"
said her caretakers
they all ganged up
the grandchildren said,
"she's making it up."
The doctor said,
"she's hallucinating."
The daughter-in-law
demanded proof
as though it is possible
to produce a receipt
for pain
her son fed her pills.
They put my bed next to hers
so I could listen to her
whimper all night
afraid of contamination
one night, I offered her
a Band-Aid
I was only seven
what did I know
I said, "Here, Nani
take this
and be done with it."
She died
twenty-eight years later
her pain done with.

Puzzle

I am
piecing
together
a puzzle,
a puzzle
a puzzle
this is your head
this is my hand
where is your neck?
I read
in the newspaper
a woman
died
of strangulation.
What should I do now?

Smoked Out

When the flame
lit in your eyes
your hands exploded
ablaze with desire.
I was afraid
I knew so little
but you insisted
to light suns in my body.
Yes, it's only the body I remember
tongues, fingers,
fingers, tongues
cold lips of the night
on my breast
and suddenly for no reason
I want to talk of fire
I want to burn your body
in my eyes
I want to see
the begrimed scales of your skin
blacken
I want to set a match
to your hands
so they never singe
another woman
they never see
the beginning of another love.

SHERAZAD JAMAL

Making of a Cultural Schizophrenic

Excitement ...
a new place, a new beginning
a life like in the American films
gold dust and man-made stars
illuminating the landscape
all waiting for us
across the Atlantic Ocean.

Snow for the first time ...
What will it be like
cold wet melting on my nose
making snowmen
just like a character in an Enid Blyton book
the tropical three
my brothers and me.

My parents have left already
we are with my uncle
who seems to have forgotten

what it is like to be young
scolding, no playing in the house.
When will we be with mum and dad again?

The call comes
put the children
on the plane to Vancouver.
Fighting, arguing at long distance rates
with the family's patriarchal hierarchy,
my father, youngest son, talks back.
Send the children now
we have been assured everything will be taken care of.
Have you gone crazy? they have no visas
we are not putting your children in danger.
Taro maguj kharab thaygyun chhe?
The wives cluck their tongues
and shake their heads nervously:
should we let them go to Canada?
look, they have only been away for
four months and already they have begun
to forget the old ways.

In two weeks we are on the plane
to Vancouver
embarking on an adventure
the tropical three
have never been on a plane before.
Ironically (i remember) Bob Hope is on the screen
on his way to Africa.

It is a long ride
almost a whole day in the air
floating above billowing clouds
as close to heaven as i have ever been.

Anticipation builds
see mum and dad again
see our new home
see how beautiful it is from the night sky
diamonds glittering shimmering along the coastline
paradise.

We are taken to a special room.
Wait, your parents will be with you soon
they sound different, the Canadians
not at all like the English
more American really.
We'd expected English accents
more like ours
Canada being a part of the commonwealth and all.

We thank them
someone asks how our flight was
are we tired
no, the tropical three are in
tip top condition but feeling a little
grotty and sweaty
why are they looking at us funny?
did we say something wrong?

Reunited finally with mum and dad
there are tears of joy
even from my father
whom i have never seen cry before
why do they both look so tired?

On the aerobus to our new home
my parents have warned us
it is not our home in Nairobi
a three bedroom bungalow
floating in the sea of land
room enough for the tropical three
to play cricket and soccer
to run among the trees laden with passion fruit and
tangerines
to dig up white ant queens
to catch chameleons
to create worlds of our own.

The bus races through this new city
lights are on everything
does it ever sleep?
We stop at the Vancouver Hotel
to take a taxi, no — a cab
the boot of the car, no — trunk
is filled with our luggage
the taxi driver asks where we are from
we tell him proudly
we have just arrived in this land
our new land
to help us celebrate, he does not take his fare.

Our first meal in Canada
hamburgers eaten under golden arches
unlike anything we have ever had before.

And now home
a high-rise tower
where are the open stretches of land?

We have never lived fifty feet in the air before
a one bedroom apartment for five
dingy dark brown melancholy
floors covered in ochre carpet
the colour of diarrhea.

My parents are telling us how lucky
they were to get this place
it's owned by Indians, you see
the others don't readily accept
Indian people in their buildings
apparently it has something to do
with the smell of our cooking ...

We are all tense
and i don't know why
my brother flicks on the TV
Images ...
Flip Wilson, a familiar face from VOK
"turn that thing off"
my father snaps at him
the TV is silent
only the sound of my mother's weeping
fills the room.

Slowly the story comes out
how they have been living
out of a suitcase
from room to room
eating on *cheuro* and water some nights
scraping together
the last pennies of their travelling allowance
and their hopes for the future.

Finding work has not been easy
everyone wants "Canadian experience"
a nice way of saying
i'm sorry
but you are the wrong colour for the job
my father once ran restaurants
now he slices onions
he, too, is forced to weep
my mother would rather die
than see him lose his dignity.

My first day at school
school back home was a joy
filled with
learning, playing, running on grassy fields
with the equatorial sun warming my face
and my heart.

But i am surrounded by concrete playgrounds
and the sun here is cold.

My father accompanies me
i clutch his hand tightly
relying on his strength
to help me face the unknown
i look up to his face
and he smiles at me
reassuringly.

i am nervous and scared
i am told i will have to repeat a year
a decision based

not on my actual intelligence
but on my age.
"born in 1963? — grade 4"
it is done
they do not want to see past my face
are all coloured immigrants considered stupid
until proven intelligent?

The grade four classroom
i see my face replicated in half of the seats
nervous uncertain faces ...

Then in the playground
it begins
"Hey, Paki! Go home!
What was it like in the African jungle, Paki,
swinging with Tarzan?
Hey, she's Cheetah —
Ape-face, Ape-face!"

i am numb in shock
i don't even know what "Paki" means
i feel only hostility and hate
alone alone alone
an island in a sea of faces
confused hurt brown ones
and sneering jeering white ones
taking pleasure in tearing off our wings
one by one.

i race home for comfort
my brothers are there but
they have not fared well either

only two years of high school to do
that's their consolation
a wedge between the tropical three forms.

My mother
home from an exhausting day of legal language
typing mortgage documents and
repressing her identity
i weep endlessly
"i want to go home ...
i hate this place ... they hate me
they call me names."

My mother cradles my head in her lap
stroking my hair and
whispering comforting things
she lifts my face to hers
"We can't go home ... this is our home now.
We all will have to learn to get along here."
Why are her eyes so lifeless?

Back to school again
so much to learn
but nothing to do with school books.

They make fun of us all
they follow us home
they scream names at us
they throw rocks at us
they beat us up
waving baseball bats
in halo-like circles
around their heads.

Quickly the first lessons of survival:
stick with your own kind
and run like hell.

My parents the pacifists
eventually, reluctantly
advocate violence
the tropical three have not heard them
speak this way before

strangely, it works
we must meet abuse with abuse
violence with violence
not with reason.

There is nothing reasonable about this situation.

We learn gradually to cope
we have each other
our communal bonds, our religion
we have become
more religious, more traditional
than ever back home
to block the pain of our differences
by embracing it
strength seems to come from
our collective invocation to Allah.

god help us all

In dimly lit grey apartments
we gather

shadows of our former selves
sharing humiliation, dislocation, alienation, pain
and loneliness
the only time we can speak freely
in our own language,
in our own voices
and be understood
beyond the words

We learn to split personalities
we become chameleons
we take on different accents
we dress differently
we change our names
we meet all expectations
we are quiet and keep our heads down
we are good coloured people
we don't want no trouble
in the sanctuary of our homes
we are closer to what we were before
but not quite ... there is something missing
we can relax a little
but not totally
will we ever feel at home here?

Gaps begin to grow between us
generation gaps
gender gaps
all seem acute
identity and belonging is unclear
big fights with my family
traditional expectations unmet
i am affected by feminism

which offers choices and freedoms
not allowed in our traditions,
life-savers in this era of turmoil.

My parents don't understand these
"Canadian" ways
it was never like this back home
no dating, no kissing, no holding hands
dhowkis — are loose, fast
do you want to be like them?
dhowkas — well you know they're interested in only one thing,
i must marry within the community
a nice boy from a good family
like my mother and her mother before her
for continuity
we must survive.

Yet i am surrounded by media representations
of the forbidden
only, none of the women look like me
blonde blue-eyed creamy-white-skinned
men look at me like
i have leprosy, untouchable
like my forefathers
before converting to Islam
i am on the outside looking in
wishing hoping craving
to be accepted as one of them
and knowing it will never be so.

My brothers fare differently
their schizophrenia seems not as great as mine
they are exotica for some

blond blue-eyed creamy-white-skinned women
but they cannot transcend certain barriers
the tradition holds us all in check

We are raised with the scars of
apartheid.
My parents have ingrained in them
and in us
respect for authority
blond blue-eyed creamy-white-skinned
authority. Don't complain,
at least in Canada they let us walk
on the same side of the street with them
eat in the same restaurants with them
and shit in the same toilets as them.

We are fooled by these liberal gestures
this racism from pallor to colour
like a coy woman
in an Urdu *ghazal*
the object of her lover's desire and agony
she teases him to the point of pain
engaging him in countless games of Swaal-Jwaab
but she and he both know where
the real power lies
he will never truly be one with her.

SHEILA JAMES

Indian Woman/English Man

(Toronto, 1992)

ON GOOD DAYS WE WALK hand in hand. We pass little kisses
to each other through knowing smiles and familiar gestures.
We speak in breathless whispers and longing sighs. On good
days we indulge in the history of us. We remember the first
day we met, our first dance, our first date. We remember the
first time we kissed and, in detail, the first time we made love.
We even remember the first time we fought and then, gratefully, how we made up.

On good days, we pull the photo albums from the shelf
and we indulge in the history of us. We see ourselves on our
wedding day: you white as a ghost, nervous and uncomfortable in your black tux; me, confident and proud, wearing a
frothy white veil which brings out the ebony hue of my skin.
On the good days our photographs support the theory that
opposites attract. In fact it is a truth which cannot be disput-
ed. Together, forever, just the two of us.

On bad days, we sleep in separate rooms. The processed
voices on the television replace our animated conversation,

and we desperately focus on trivial domestic chores to avoid each other's eyes. When silence falls, it's not peaceful and tranquil, but heavy and oppressive. It is the muted and strained rotation of our minds wondering what went wrong.

On bad days, your white skin blinds me like the harsh light from a bare bulb, and the superstructures of your world tower above me and block me out. My brown skin becomes a burnt-out shell providing shelter for my lost soul, pathetically grasping at the flimsy threads of my past. Then the photographs appear stark, our memories become painful, and I recount the history of us.

Wasn't it your great-great-grandfather who forced my great-grandmother's body into a cannon, then fired it like a live cannon ball through the air and into the masses, to teach them a lesson about resisting British rule?

Wasn't it your grandfather who so generously saved my grandmother from her pagan gods and claimed her soul for the mission of his white Jesus?

Wasn't it your father who took credit for educating my mother about Shakespeare, Dickens and Darwin, but refused to recognize her abilities, making certain she would never earn a decent wage in his country?

Wasn't it your brother who, while investing millions overseas, travelled across the ocean to throw pennies at my sister, buying the privilege to invade her malnourished and childlike body just so that he could live out his erotic/exotic fantasies?

And ... wasn't it you who charmed, seduced, and coerced me into believing in your wonderful western world, convincing me that I would be treated as an equal, when all along you knew I would live forever under your thumb?

On bad days, this history drops like a bomb on our home, dividing and destroying everything we created with love and courage. And for a moment, my rage reduces you to tears and the sources for your power and privilege are exposed:

my great-great-grandmother's labour
my great-grandmother's blood
my grandmother's spirit
my mother's mind
my sister's body
my innocence

On bad days, it is with this knowledge that I reach for you ... and you still wonder why I like to be on top.

She Will Keep Coming Back

(April 1994, Hyderabad, India)

No matter how many ways they try to kill her
                    She will keep coming back

Not as a goddess, her spirit redeemed
    But as a god-less preacher
            a guilt-less thief
                    a rebel princess
                            a bandit queen

They tried to kill her at her husband's funeral pyre
Fanatical choruses reached the sky
   The louder she'd scream
   The louder they'd try
   To disguise her pain as they all stood by
   and watched her body being burned alive
   Whispering they say she was pushed in
   by her son her next of kin
   he shall inherit his father's property
   and her death will bring honour to the family!

   For religious leaders and politicians agree
   she has a right to be
   devoted to god
   and do her wifely duty

They tried to kill her on her wedding night
For bringing in less then she was worth
   or ... for daring to walk proudly in the light
   or ... for simply being born woman on this earth

   One flame, one can of kerosene
   will hide the evidence but not her screams
   the neighbours heard they saw her tomb
   a heap of ashes displaced by the broom

   The newspapers read
   she took her life
   a much loved daughter
   a much loved wife

   Knowing this
   fathers still stand in line

and pay for a wedding
and funeral ... combined.

They tried to kill her in the womb
a test that said her life was doomed
    An appointment made
    a dowry saved
    some question this but most insist
    her worthless life will not be missed

    And for her mother
    how many times
    must she spread her legs
    and remove the signs

    that she has conceived
    again and again
    a girl child
    whom she cannot defend

No matter how many ways they try to kill her

        SHE WILL KEEP COMING BACK

Not as a goddess her spirit redeemed
    but as a god-less leader
        a guilt-less thief
            a rebel princess
                a bandit queen

with 1000 daggers and 1000 smiles to avenge the MURDER of
her past lives.

❦ SHEILA JAMES ❦

From Promiscuity to Celibacy: A Creative Piece on Sexuality

(Toronto, 1991)

I AM A SOUTH ASIAN SLUT! Raised a dutiful daughter of Indian immigrant medical doctors, I realized early in life that I would fail to meet the professional and personal expectations of my parents. You see, I aspire to nothing more than to have a good ... no, a great, sex life.

My obsession with sex began when I discovered the "dirty" pictures in the *National Geographic* magazines (you know the ones). Anyway, I would covet the magazines, take them to my room and greedily devour them with my six year old eyes. Often I'd share my photo treasures with other children wondering if they felt those exciting tingles at seeing full breasts and the dark nipples of the African woman. I dreamt that one day my breasts would emerge so dark and full, but that dream has yet to reach fruition. Well, my penchant for *National Geographic* came to a halt when I was caught red-handed by my shocked and disappointed mother. "Shameful girl" echoes over and over in my head and the magazines were moved to my parents' office. This incident, however, didn't dissuade me one bit. By putting pen to paper, I realized that I could create my own anatomically correct characters. Pictures of naked bodies surfaced all over our house: on the telephone directory, in my sister's scribblers, on desk tops and walls. My art, of course, was quite naïve. You see, I knew little about sex and even less about sexual intercourse. It was not until I discovered the *Kama Sutra* in my parents' bedside table that the world of fucking was opened to me.... Was it 69 or 169 positions? I examined each drawing one by one, imagining my perfect, puritanical parents engaging in such activity. Well,

well, well ... With their unspoken go-ahead, my fantasies flourished.

I entered my own fantasies as a super sex star! Naturally, I became well-endowed. Unnaturally, I became a blonde. Why not? All the sex objects on TV, film and magazines were blond-haired and blue-eyed. I figured I could adjust the colour in my head to fit the role. Who would ever know? As my fantasies became more detailed, I sought new inspiration. Where else could I find detail but in my parents' medical journals. This is where I first glimpsed the female genitalia. As non-traditional casting was not yet in vogue; all the photography models were white-skinned. I saw pink vagina, pink lips, and white asshole. "Hmmm ... so this is what it looks like." I decided a self-examination was long overdue. You can imagine my surprise when, at nine years old, I squatted over a small hand mirror to discover that my hot pink vagina was modestly covered by purplish lips and leering at me from behind was the wrinkly eye of my little brown asshole. It was mocking me, saying, "ha ha we fooled you!" Did I really think that my genitals would resemble the ones in the photos? Talk about internalized racism.

The years went by and puberty hit. Pimples, strange proportions and other teenage problems took me under ... to the world of my fantasies. I had thousands of scenarios featuring different people, different places and different positions. One of my favourites was the fantasy where I became a high-class hooker. Of course I knew nothing about the reality of prostitution. I simply associated the profession with lots of sex, which I wanted, and lots of money, which I also wanted. Luckily for my parents, I didn't take my vocational dream too seriously. Problem was, I was bad in business. I ended up sleeping with people for free! Well ... not exactly free. There are always small paybacks. Like flattery, for instance. I discovered very quickly that the fewer clothes I wore the more compliments I'd receive. It got so that I'd be on a date, stark naked, saying "Ah, gee you don't mean it. Ah go on ..." I guess I should add that I experienced my first date, first kiss, and first lay all in the same night. I was nineteen years old, in university, and extremely horny. You see, being a South Asian girl living in a predominantly white, middle-class town, and having a curfew at eight thirty pm minimized my chances of getting a date, let alone a boyfriend. But don't feel sorry for me. My early twenties proved quite active.

Sex soon became a substitute for everything: food, drugs, exercise, recreation, attention, affection and unfortunately, love. It was a big ego booster and I shared my ego with everyone. Yes, I've been around the block enough times to know the neighbourhood and the drivers have been of both sexes. No, gender was never an issue. I lusted after men and I lusted after women, so please indulge a little generalization. My experience has shown me that men are easier lays than women. Put it this way; I've slept with most of my male friends and tried to sleep with most of my female friends. Ah, but this shouldn't come as a surprise in such an outwardly heterosexual and heterosexist world.

Some friends say I should identify myself as bisexual, but I'd rather just call myself sexual. After all, I do have sex with myself and I must admit that I am the most willing, reliable and faithful partner I've ever had. Fifteen years and the flame still burns. Of course, sex toys help: dildos, erotic literature, and the old hand mirror. In nights of self-absorbed passion, I'd often hold the mirror above my vulva pretending I was my own lusty lover. What a change from the medical journal days.

Yes, a lot of things have changed. I decided to commit myself to a year of celibacy. During this time, I reflected upon my sexual history and how it was somehow shaped by the images in the environment around me. I had internalized racism and sexism to such a degree that my way of belonging was to be sexually acceptable to almost anyone. My needs propelled me down a reckless road. There was both fun and frustration along the way but most of the time I felt I had lost control of the wheel. The year of celibacy not only helped me to develop amazing self-control, but self-satisfaction as well. After lots of gentle caressing and self-discipline, I've come to love my cunt. Now I see sexuality as a jewel; sometimes undervalued and given away, other times over-controlled and locked up, and all too often forced from us against our will. In some hands, the jewel is dull. In other hands, it emanates light and beauty. But as long as it remains in the right hands, mine, it works like a gem.

NILAMBRI SINGH GHAI

Your Name

I do not utter your name
for you are meant to be a deity.
All men are gods, they say,
for the women who marry them.

I do not utter your name
lest the air around listens
to the silent voice
waiting for you to come back
from I dare not ask where.

I do not utter your name
before your parents, your uncles,
your brothers, and everyone else
that you know, and I don't,
lest they misconceive
my overtures.

I do not utter your name
lest my youthful voice and body
attract others by the similarity
of a name.

I would not utter your name
even if I longed
to hold your hand
close to my body
that you have never really seen.

I should not utter your name
when I see anger in your eyes
because I did not wash and cook,
because your mother was upset,
because I over-stayed the visit
at my parents' home,
because I talk too much,
because I reveal secrets
meant only for the family,
because I crave too much,
and ask for too much,
am never satisfied.

I should not utter your name
even when your hand rises
against my face in total abandonment;
I must not utter your name
nor must I strike back.

Eventually, some day,
when the breeze is still,
and the sky is clear,
your mother is expecting

her regular gifts
from my parents,
I shall utter your name,
and in the quiet of that night
when you shall ask:
"What's in a name?"
I'll answer:
"Everything!"

Woman/Man

I loved a man
who loved me as
a woman
who thought
of me
as someone
to love
for what I was
and not for what
I could or could not do.

I loved this woman/man
man/woman
he/she clasped me
in his hands
till such time as he felt
he was over, and I could see
the woman in him disappear
to be replaced by
cold, spent strength.

Rano

Shy, sad, veiled, widowed
she walks through the village
scared she may be seen
even by her own shadow
and raped. Her life subsists
in him who deigned
to marry and protect one such as her
whom he promises to strike again
if she persists in coming
between him and his bottle,
to show to those he most accepts
that he cares not to be had
by common admonishings
of an over-zealous wife.
Till one day he dies
suddenly, as though to take away
deliberately the blows that made up
life for her in a strange
unglamorous way,
leave her to marry his brother
whom she had nursed
along with her son.
And all the while her body
is not her own — it belongs
to them,
their whims and fanciful decisions.
Rano still lives and survives
in a world that does not want her
and yet needs her to produce children
and serve its men.

*This poem is based on RS Bedi's story of a Punjabi woman forced
to marry her young brother-in-law after the death of her husband.*

Hierarchy

There was power
in your words
that made me feel
powerless and yet
sick at myself
for I had failed to do
what I'd told myself I would.

There was anger in your words
that made me lose the anger
I had summoned up
to confront yours.

There was delight in your heart
for my inability
my incapacity
my inadequacy.
There was success in your heart
due to my failure,
and there was sorrow in mine
to see what you had made of yourself.

God

God is he for some
a she for others
nothing for who knows what
to make of a genderless
faceless deity.

There is a god they say
and tell all generations,
a male god and a few
female goddesses perhaps
but a supreme male deity
looking down on his creation
relating to half the world
in patrimonious harmony.
The other half meantime
enclosed by a gender unknown
to mankind, seeking corners
for the best view behind veils
and control of renowned beauty
to capture demonic souls
through seduction
and suggestive rape.

VEENA GOKHALE

Reveries of a Riot

THE RIOT HAS BEEN RAGING outside Mira's window for more than two days.

The window is large and square. Lacy white curtains frame it on the inside. A second set of curtains in rough-textured *khaddar* patterned with maroon and yellow stripes is used to protect the lace from the searing heat of the sun and to keep out the glare on reclining Sunday afternoons when Mira reads, dozes, embroiders or listens to Hindustani classical music, a lazy softness of a stretching cat stealing over her.

The window has remained shut now for two days. So has their front door. Both unmoving as the curfew flickers on and off outside like a light bulb gone crazy. Mira is nearly out of fresh milk and running low on vegetables.

During this time of enforced rest, Mira returns to the window again and again. She sits at some distance from it curled up on the over-stuffed sofa or straight up in the old rocking-chair. Or down on the carpet, knees drawn to her chin, contemplating the window. The window has become not something to look out of but something to look at.

On the first day of the riot, Mira and her husband Mihir were getting ready to go to work when they heard shouts, the sound of running feet, breaking glass and then a gunshot. They rushed to the window, Mihir putting out a restraining hand to prevent Mira from sticking her head too far out.

All they saw at first were three men running away and broken glass on the pavement opposite their apartment building. Either the tailoring shop or the bakery or both must have been vandalized.

Mira felt Mihir draw in his breath sharply. It was then that she saw the body sprawled face-down on the pavement at the edge of the street.

Mira's first commonplace thought was: this is like the movies. She expected to see a thin trickle of blood run out from under the man's feet into the open drain, turning the brown sewage water to a darker hue.

But there was no blood that day or the next, just distant shouts and screams.

The next morning, the contents of the tailoring shop and the bakery — shelves and counters, trays and sewing machines, chairs and curtains, knickknacks — had been dented, broken and thrown on the pavement. Some of the things had spilled onto the street.

The attack must have occurred at dawn or very early in the morning, before they had woken up and taken positions beside the window. They had missed the action.

They had heard more than they had seen, their view confined to the narrow strip of the road, pavement and housefronts, while their ears extended like antennae, picking up distorted air waves from all around.

On the first day, they had felt compelled to spend long hours at the window to monitor the riot on the radio and the television (which weren't giving much away). And the telephone. It was a day punctuated by quick visits from the neighbours — speculative conversations, forced little jokes, lamentations on the state of the government, politics, the country and the world, hastily exchanged reassurances.

They had said among themselves over and over that things could not go on like this. Tempers had to cool. People need to come back to their senses.

The anger and hate would be snuffed out by death. The smell of death filling the streets and the houses, spreading over the city like an oil spill contaminating the sea. Anger and hate would be diluted by the wailing of frightened children, the ritualized mourning of widows, the public grief of relatives — loud, harsh, unrelenting.

There was the police force, and the army. The army would know how to handle a situation like this, even if the police failed. Community groups too would play a role, surely, going door to door, counselling, consoling, pleading, haranguing.

Peace would come. It might take some time but it would descend, eventually, like a soothing late-monsoon shower, gentle and fragrant.

Meanwhile it was best to stay indoors. Stay calm. In control. Do the ordinary, everyday things — cooking, eating, sleeping — that would blanket the insanity which had taken over the streets. Keep the thoughts from scattering in unseemly directions.

On that near-normal first day of the riot, Mira walked around their spacious livingroom, over-furnished at the edges, examining the many things — inherited, gifted, bought, picked up, and others that seemed to have turned up on their own — with a solemn interest.

She spent quite a while at the bookshelves, specially the one that held all the old, mouldy books that smelled so good. Here was *Wuthering Heights* nestling next to *War and Peace. The Trial* cheek-and-jowl with *The Old Man and the Sea.*

Books by Agatha Christie and PG Wodehouse.

And the books on Hindu spirituality — the Upanishads, the Bhagavadgita, the writings of Ramkrishna Paramhans, Vivekanand, Shri Aurobindo and the Mother. These books had belonged to Mira's father-in-law, whom she had never met. He had passed away when Mihir was just ten years old.

A newer and smaller bookshelf was devoted to Graham Greene, Gabriel Garcia Marquez, Italo Calvino, Toni Morrison, Salman Rushdie, Bapsi Sidhwa, Amitav Ghosh and others.

The two remaining bookshelves could have been labeled "his" and "hers." One held Mihir's books on engineering, management and cricket, plus a smattering of poetry in English and Gujarati.

Mira's bookshelf contained scholarly volumes on sociology. She had started the collection when she had embarked on her Master of Social Work degree at the Tata Institute of Social Sciences, and had meticulously added to it through the six subsequent years of her professional life in academia.

Here you could also find cookery books — the regional cuisine from the many Indian states — and pattern books on embroidery, craft books, books on feminism, and old magazines — *Eve's Weekly*, in its more radical avatar, *Manushi*, *Filmfare*, and the *Economic and Political Weekly*. Half a dozen Hindi novels and a few volumes of *Abhilasha*, a Hindi literary quarterly.

There was so much that they had brought with them when they married and so much more they had acquired through the five years of their marriage — coffee tables, and coffee table books, wooden screens, flower vases, painted pottery, terra-cotta ashtrays, handicrafts, clocks, sketches and posters, photographs, records and cassettes, letters....

Mira had enjoyed yelling through the bedroom door at Mihir: do-you-remember-such-and-such-thing-event-person?

Mihir had come into the drawing room for a while, and they had laughingly recalled the histories and biographies of the various objects till Mihir, tired of the game, had settled in the bedroom with the latest issue of *Business India*, and Mira had fallen once again into a silent contemplation of the window.

On the second day of the riot, there were no visits from the neighbours or phone calls from friends, as though the event had gone from being a collective tragedy to a personal failure which had to be dealt with in harrowing aloneness, sealed indoors, exiled into the self.

On the second day, Mihir stayed in the bedroom, Mira in the livingroom. The violent fight they had had the night before drove them to carve out their separate spheres and stay within their isolated but still-connected spaces.

There hadn't been very much else to do but look at the window and its perfect symmetry. The white encasement, slightly scratched and chipped in places. The curtains half drawn back. The play of light against delicate lace.

The panes, dusty but secure. Whole, when there were so many shattered windows on their street, in their city. So much glittering, crunchy glass everywhere.

Whole. What a wonderful word. Treacherous though. Watch out for that one. Take away the "w" and a gaping wound opens. An external wound you think at first. Superficial. Easily healed. But a second look reveals that the knife has cut through the layers of skin to reach the vital organs, now a bloody, implacable mess, threatening to break through to the surface to reveal the hopelessness of the affliction.

What a wonderful, whole window. Watching it was both a delight and a torment. Wanting it to stay intact. Wanting it to shatter. Who were the lucky ones? Who had got it right?

Those whose windows had been broken? Or those who had found refuge behind their unblemished windows?

It was on the eve of Holi, the night when Holika, the demoness — Pralhad's tormentor — is consigned to the flames, that Mira had been entranced by a bonfire once, a long time ago.

The boys had built a huge bonfire in the field in front of Mira's house. Mira had watched them building it all evening, knowing that something significant was to come, but without a clue to what it might be.

The bonfire had been set alight after dark, by the light of lanterns — exciting, shadowy things in themselves. A roaring fire took hold with everyone milling around it, singing, dancing and eating sweets.

Mira did not join the festivities. She sat on the grass — a chubby girl with glasses — watching the flames rise and lick the sky, turning her world into a blaze, while the piercing heat turned her insides rosy warm and liquid. Later her mother had half dragged, half carried her home.

Still Mira watched the flames from her bedroom window, her mind blank, the fire consuming her from inside out, making her whole.

She had fallen asleep at her vigil by the window and woken up early as the first light of the day had crept into her eyes through shuttered eyelids.

As soon as her eyes opened Mira looked out of the window, expecting to see the fire. It was gone. Mira's heart started to beat hard. She rushed out of the house in her rubber slippers and pyjamas, knowing her mother would scold her if she found out, and ran, panting, half-falling, feeling a little sick, to the spot where the bonfire had been.

A perfect circle of ash, charred twigs and burnt grass stood in the field. As Mira walked into it, the acrid ashy smell filled her to choking and crumbling ashes, powdery soft and still warm, tickled the edges of her feet.

Looking up, Mira saw the arching blue sky go from pink to gold. It was immense, whole, as the fire had been. Bending down she grabbed fistfuls of ash. She had preserved that ash in a toffee tin for many years after that.

The fascination with the window was less innocent. But there was no option: the entrancement had to run its course.

Blood. It would have been nice to have seen some. Snarling red, viscous. Bubbling as if in anger. Simmering as if full of spite. What use a riot or a fight without the redness, the richness of real blood?

It would have been good to see a stone, stones, strike the window panes. Enter the livingroom and fall with a reverberating thud that shook the somnolent apartment.

It would have been good to see the glass crack, the pane turn into an intricate spider's web. While the other shattered and fell to the floor, tinkling.

Shards of glass everywhere. Glass, pure and beautiful. What use a riot or a fight without broken glass, without the hardness, sharpness, the clarity of glass?

But there had been no blood.

There had never, it seemed, been any *real* blood in Mira's life, unless one counted tame menstrual blood, stale and sour-smelling, as real blood. More real to her than her own blood was the tomato-ketchup blood of the countless Hindi movies that Mira had grown up on.

At first, the blood spilled on screen appeared to have a good reason to be there. It was spilled in the name of righteousness, honour, justice, love, filial devotion. But as the years rolled on, the blood-baths got more and more senseless, random and gory. The films were holding up mirrors to the reality around them.

Mira and her friends started seeing these movies less and

less as time passed because they seemed to have nothing to do with *their* ideas, *their* motivations, *their* lives. The movies had created their own universe and occupied an orbit that did not overlap with the space that defined Mira's life.

But as the first day of the riot had started to fade into night, Mira had felt her blood coursing through her veins once again, after a long time indeed. She had experienced it as a warm, lively thing, intent on action.

She couldn't figure out what had triggered off this unfreezing of her blood and her spirit, which had brought on the desperate urge to let her innards spill out through her mouth, her sole weapon.

Words had spewed out of Mira with a damning ferocity that night when everything had seemed under control in the beginning. All that time she had believed that the violence outside was an external event, unreal and transient. It had nothing to do with her, with Mihir — their ideas, their motivations, their lives.

They would move, Mihir had said. They had been searching for a flat now for over six months. They had been too picky. That's why they hadn't found anything. They had to be realistic. They had to compromise. They would settle for a half-way decent place in a nice locality. They would leave here as soon as they could.

"And what about us? Do you think that we will solve any of that by moving?"

"Don't start on that now, Mira. Not tonight of all nights. Please."

Flames licked at the corners of Mira's mind.

Flames and fire, so central to Indian life and death. The ancient fascination that endures. Sacred fire, ultimate purifier, made profane by *suttee* and bride burning. The rites and wrongs of fire still endure.

The body is consumed by fire to be made whole. Fire unlocks the spirit which merges with the whole. Fire is not so much death as it is purification and after-life. So self immolation still endures — suicide and self expression, an end and a new beginning rolled eerily into one.

The rioters had overturned three buses and set them ablaze on the main road not far from where Mira lived. That must have been some bonfire!

Flames licked at the corners of Mira's mind and she blazed with words.

Afterwards, after her eruption into angry utterances and Mihir's wordy counter-attack, Mira felt empty and slack, de-muscled, limp.

It was as if a great wind had blown through their flat, whirled all the objects around, shaken them up and set them back in their place, cleansed.

She felt she did not need to talk to Mihir ever again. This had been her first real conversation with him. And it had explained their life together with the geometric precision of the circle of ash left behind by the great bonfire.

As a child Mira had seen practically no anger or violence in her home. Her parents seemed always calm, though her father seemed a little sad at times and her mother would get somewhat testy. There appeared to be no quarrels or disagreements between them. They had chosen consciously to turn away from overt expression.

Things did not change very much in her adult life which seemed more or less like a seamless continuation of her tranquil childhood.

Before Mira and Mihir had found this flat, they had lived for a couple of months in a friend's apartment where they had had to suffer a violent neighbour.

Shouts and screams, the sounds of banging doors and

falling things, whimpers and sobs emanated at odd hours from the neighbouring apartment. Perhaps they hadn't been all that loud, but in the hushed silence of her temporary home, which had echoed the hollow quiet of her parents house, the sounds had the impact of gunshots fired at a distance. Mira remembered thinking that some day perhaps the bullets would pierce the walls of her own home.

Standing at their window Mira would see the man storm out of the apartment building after a virulent-sounding quarrel, get into the car and drive away noisily, leaving behind a swirl of dust. Sometimes, though less often, the woman would walk out of the house, a little unsteady, her *pallu* wrapped tightly around her head, dragging a sobbing child with her, to hail a rickshaw as it rounded a corner and disappear in a cloud of dust.

Through all this Mihir assured Mira again and again that they would move soon. They were spending all their after-work hours looking for a house; they were bound to find something. He appeared to get used to the situation but Mira couldn't stop herself from listening and looking out for their neighbours all the time.

She started leading a double life, lurking, in her mind, through the rooms of her neighbours' house, a ghost haunted by an intense and unnatural curiosity, even as she sat down to dinner with Mihir, or brought out her embroidery books in the drawing room or watched Mihir wrestle with the Rubic's cube.

That was the feeling she experienced once again as the riot raged outside their window. As she sat in her cosy little home leafing through glossy magazines, she was a ghost slipping through the restless streets.

Now she was part of the crowd that jeered and cheered, hurled stones and abuse and set things alight. (What delight in seeing the flames rise high and lick the sky!) The crowd that had become a single moving, tensing, preying beast, intent on action....

Now she was in a dingy, wayside tea stall, listening to the rabble-rouser at the upturned table, his speech and spittle darting back and forth between him and his audience, people listening, forgetting their companions, the tea turning tepid in their cups, Someone whistled. Someone clapped. "Kya hero aadmi hai...."

Then she was moving down a street where everything was burning — the houses, the shops, the cars, the people — and she was dodging falling rafters and flying sparks, walking around the blazing bodies rolling on the ground trying to quell the flames, hanging on to life in the throes of death, she was shrinking from burning limbs that were thrust at her from writhing heaps. And everywhere the stench of burning flesh ...

She was on a street now where there were no people and no fires, only glass everywhere, crushed glass covering the sidewalk and road and the walls of buildings, the whole world so crystalline and beautiful, blinding her with its brilliance.

Then she was on her own street which had been all cleaned up. There were people going about their business unsmiling, silent.

Mira walked along quickly and uneasily down the street and towards her house, knowing that if someone made one small false move, the facade of normalcy would crumble and there would be glass on the street and the sound of running feet and shouts and gunshots.

They all had to be very, very careful. She knew that with an absolute certainty that made her break out in sweat. What if it were she who did something wrong?

She felt a scream forming at the base of her throat and rising slowly, and then she was at the entrance of her building, her self-control deserting her as soon as she was inside the door, making her run up the hollow-sounding wooden stair, till she collided into a man who was going down the stairs.

As she brushed against him Mira got a whiff of his sweat mingled with that other body smell, unmistakable despite her fear and the total darkness that enveloped the staircase. This man was her first lover, who had been at one time as big as the bonfire in Mira's life, blotting out everything else.

He seemed to recognize her and paused, though he had been in a great hurry a second ago. For a moment they withdrew into them-selves, preparing for the encounter. Then they embraced.

Tongues of fire licked at Mira's skin. Her body felt translucent, cool, like fine glass.

He kissed her roughly on her mouth. He had a week-old beard that scratched her face. He hadn't had the time to shave or hadn't bothered to. He seemed agitated, his body too-warm, trembly. Mira clung closer to him and pushed her tongue into his feverish mouth.

He had been there, out on the streets, rioting. His clothes and skin were street-stained. Nothing else could explain his disturbed state.

Perhaps at first he had just been a passerby on a mindless errand, walking hurriedly down a street. Perhaps he had left his quiet side-street and walked onto a main street, into the eye of an inferno, surrounded suddenly by a throng of angry, shouting, crazed people throwing stones and hitting out at whatever they could find. Being of an excitable nature, the impressionable young man that he was, perhaps he had been drawn in by the crowd, a participant rather than spectator in the random violence that creat-ed its purpose as it went along.

As Mira slipped her hand into his she felt the grainy texture of mud on it.

The images of the streets outside coalesced into a single flame and burned in Mira's mind. She felt as if he shared the flame. That in fact he was fueling and brightening it as his body heat seeped into her. As they kissed, breathing chaotically, Mira pushed hard against him, wanting the street-sweat, mud-violence; the feverish hunger-anger of his tongue to infuse her being as well.

He led Mira by hand to the top of the building to the little recess, musty, cobwebbed, stacked with discarded junk, that led to the terrace, which was locked.

Half undressing, they clung, clawed, bit, thrust, tugged, stroked each other in a frenzy of love and despair. As he took her standing up, Mira felt his calloused hands (what had he been doing with his butter-smooth hands, soft and gentle in her memory?) grasp her hair, gather it in his fist, and pull her head back, hard. Pain, black and deep, washed over her as she came and came.

Now she was no longer apart, but a part of the riot, and would always be, with a part of the riot inside her forever.

He left her outside her flat. A brush of lips against her earlobe, a hand momentarily tightening around hers and he faded away. She couldn't smell him any longer. Though she could feel him still. Mira stood in the dark for a while, running her fingers over her swollen lips. Then she let herself into the apartment.

They had picked the body off the pavement that very day, the first day of the riot. Late in the afternoon an ambulance had driven up, a siren rending the air. Two policemen had got out of the van and hauled the corpse into the car. There was no blood on the man's clothes. It was not anyone they could recognize, no one they had seen before in the neighbourhood.

There were no marks on the pavement. At least nothing they could see at that distance.

Mira could picture the body lying on the cold bunk inside the ambulance which must smell depressingly of disinfectant. Perhaps they would cover him with a sheet.

What a strange corpse!

Dead bodies were covered from neck to toe in a white sheet, bedecked in garlands of flowers, their exposed faces set in response. They lay on *charpayees* held aloft by four to five men who dressed in white, freshly bathed, carried the corpses down the street followed by a procession of white-clad mourners chanting *"Ram naam satya hai."*

The man had been felled by a single bullet. They had heard just one shot. Who knows who the bullet had been meant for? Who knows how many sightless, meandering bullets had been forced to find a kill — someone who happened to be at a window, someone going about on a mundane errand, someone who had tried to duck into a doorway, some idiot with his back to the wall.

It's getting dark outside so Mira goes into the kitchen to cook some *dal-chawal.* She decides to use the two remaining onions for the dal. Pulling out the knife, she goes chop-chop-chop with it. The blade slices rhythmically through the skin to reach the heart and goes on to the other side. Soon there is a heap of finely chopped onion on the board.

Tears run down Mira's face. She wipes them inadequately with a dishcloth.

"Allah ho Akbar." Mira watches Mihir through the kitchen door as he starts up on hearing the familiar prayer call. They haven't heard it for two days. Mihir's eyes meet Mira's and turn hastily away.

There's a knock on the door. The neighbours start dropping in in quick succession. There has been no curfew today, the third day of the riot. And if the mosque has been opened again, then everything must be all right.

I can go to work tomorrow, thank god, says one neighbour, I have to finish this important report for these clients who're coming in next week. They're Japanese, you know.

Mira brews cups of tea and hands them out through the kitchen door to Mihir, leaving him to deal with the visitors. She hates him for expressing different views to different neighbours depending on their religion.

Tomorrow she would walk down the street, going around

the area where the dead man had lain, superstitious and queasy about stepping into that space, but unable to shake off a horrible curiosity that would lead her to closely examine the ground as she went by.

The bakery and the tailor shop would be repaired. The week after she would go into the bakery to buy savory *naan* bread to go with the *keema-mutter* that she makes so well.

Later, she would go into the tailor shop with her magenta silk blouse piece to have a blouse stitched in the latest style, where the tailor's wife, her *burka* thrown back over her broad, impassive face, would hand her dog-eared pattern books from under the counter.

Wearing the new blouse, her gorgeous, new Kanjivaram sari rippling and crackling around her, she would go, a week later, to her cousin's wedding, where they would not discuss the riot. The talk would centre around the decorations, the excess or simplicity of the jewellery on the women guests, the groom's income, the bride's beauty and the quality of the ice cream served at the reception.

How would she conduct herself with the baker and the tailor, her neighbours, after all, if only by chance? Would she smile effusively at them, while they, addressing her as "Behendjee," ask after Mihir Miya's health?

Or would their transactions be concluded in an aura of bewildering guilt and shame, with an absence of eye-contact and a minimum of conversation?

Suddenly Mira decides that she has to get out of the apartment, go for a walk. Opening her closet, she finds a *dopatta* and drapes it around her head. She takes off her *bindi* and sticks it on the mirror of the dressing-table.

Telling Mihir that she is going out for a while, she sweeps past him and out of the door before he has time to react.

Mira goes unhurriedly down the stairs and into the semideserted streets. They are somewhat cleaner than she had expected, though there is more than the usual load of garbage piled up at street corners. The streets are surprisingly devoid of policemen. Here and there are burnt-out shells of things that were formerly whole.

Almost all the shops are closed, and there's a plethora of them — small, individualistic shops selling fabric, clothes, shoes, toys, school goods, attar and incense, jewellery, buttons and lace, kitchenware, hardware, food, dairy products. There are shops that repair watches, leather goods, bicycles. A couple of the groceries have their doors half open.

The neighbourhood is old, the majority of the buildings dilapidated, badly in need of a coat of paint. They contrast sharply with the occasional smart new apartment building which is architecturally stark and angular. The older buildings have graceful curved balconies with wrought-iron railings and their windows and doors, composed of softly rotting wood, are framed by patterned arches, the designs either floral or geometric or a combination, looking as if they have half melted into the ancient facades.

Mira gets off the bigger and wider road and goes down a familiar *galli*, twisted and aromatic, past children playing hopscotch and skipping rope. A little girl in heavy pigtails catches her eye and smiles shyly.

She pauses as she finds herself approaching the mosque. The door to the mosque is ajar. Prayers spill out of the courtyard, into the dusky air. The minarets are outlined as inspiring silhouettes against the clear, blue sky.

Mira goes up to the door and peeps in. Inside there are a dozen odd men in white *kurta*-pyjamas and knitted skullcaps kneeling, bent over so that their heads almost touch the floor, praying. They are all grouped at the far corner of the courtyard.

The openness of the courtyard comes as a shock almost, after the circumscribed space of the apartment. Mira feels exhilarated looking at the courtyard. As she watches, the space seems to hum, extend outwards and upwards.

In the centre of the courtyard is a group of pigeons hopping and fluttering on the floor. The soft, grey bodies cut a pleasing pattern against the beautiful marble floor.

The pigeons take off and within seconds they are afloat high in the sky, flying in formation. Mira watches them till they disappear, mingling smokily into the blue-grey sky.

Suddenly she is melancholy. How limiting it is to be outside the mosque. Excluded also from the flight of the pigeons. With only the option of a linear escape — the shutting of windows and the slamming of doors?

Mira slowly makes her way back home.

UMA PARAMESWARAN

For December 6 Memorial, 1992

My sisters, my loves,
when
we circled the flame
that once was Susan, Wilma, Anne Marie,
Michele, Sonia, Geneviève;
when
we came together again and again
with our candles, other names,
but always the same pain,
to hold hands around the flame
that once was sister, lover, child;
when
we cried for women brutally slain,
and grieved we had to come so often
to hold hands around the flame,
Oh then
there was such power around us and within
that I could have reached my arms across the stars
and touched the Mother's face and said,

I am home, home at last
among my sisters, my loves,
with whom I shall one day meet in joy
as I meet here in pain.

But now
though the Mother's eyes still smile on me
from intergalactic space,
my sisters move along the halls
on the other sides of other walls.

O my sisters, my loves,
can we come together only in grief
and not in joy?

*For the Women's Centre, which needs our support all through
the year but gets it only in times of intense shared grief.*

Race

When I tied my ankle to my partner's
or pulled the gunny up to my waist
and crazily hopped to the tape,
when I gleefully carried a bag of sand or stones
or thrust the scroll in my haste
into my teammate's face instead of hand,
when I ran for the sheer joy of wind
or monsoon drizzle on my face and beat
my brothers to our mother's arms
to Dad's fond chiding that I belonged
to Hanuman's clan.
I never thought that one day I would wait
in this lovely land of endless skies
for my little ones to return safely
from school, unharassed by boys
with blond hair gelled or spiked,
their blue eyes glazed with glue,
or worse, with plain cold hatred
all faculties intact,
thrusting their fists into Krish's face,
no accident, pelting stones and eggs
by summer light on our window-panes.

My children,
sack, potato, three-legged, relay, marathon,
one hundred, two, four hundred yard dash,
that's what race once meant
and only that. But for you
that simple childhood word never was.

Mariam Khan Durrani

A Youth Rebels

A youth
rebels

A youth I am
optimistic
energetic
impatient
I am
ambitious
revolutionary
visionary
tragic
dangerous
I am
coming out   surfacing
from the core   of a beat
in the name of mutuality
and its circumstances
passing the test of time ...

of time — becoming doubtful
undoubtful of myself

in turn
leaving the nurturing
of a dependence
finding harshness and solace
of interdependence
suffering from panics and back breaks
greed, self-growth and realization

feeling demand on demand
a tug of war

yet time passes
ever still
ever lasting

in control of everything
the moral of
the story

A Youth Rebels

Shabana

"I KNOW I LOVE YOU, and I should be with you all the time. I consider you perfect, and I know I can do anything with you. I want to do everything with you, but you think that I am just a passing relationship, you don't even see me as part of your future." The exact words of my lover.

"I do see you in my future, but I always say no relationship will always be filled with happy times. I always think relationships end, sooner or later, like the seasons of nature. But I love you. You make me feel carefree and happy." My own exact words spoken to my lover.

Looking back at the conversation we had, I think this is the time when two people in love gradually blind each other. He blinded me and I blinded myself. He told himself he loved me; he fooled himself. And I always thought I loved him, but I was a fool too.

Time passes by, as I don't want to repeat or even mention the word love again. We have worn it out. We have abused it.

Oh well, you learn from the results of your, let's say mis-judgements. That's where this particular story begins. I may have amused you with the first few paragraphs, but I intend to get serious soon.

I wasn't taking that "do it yourself kit" test: I went to my physician and asked her to give me instructions. I wasn't going to do this by myself, and so secretly.

She told me I had conceived.

No immediate shock sprung inside me, though. It sure was a surprise.

Well, so much for those protective latex condoms! "Nothing's gettin' through this sucker!" my homegirl was tellin' me. Yeah, bullshit! I giggled. I really felt like laughing.

I hadn't noticed, but a shocking feeling was beginning to stab me. It was all over me.

Holy shit — my parents! This was something my parents would definitely notice. This sure wouldn't be easy to hide — I mean month by month, it'd be visible enough. I didn't like this. Panic raced inside me.

My now cold, tense face and stiff body turned to my physician.

"Thanks for your help."

"No problem. Good luck."

"Goodbye." I spoke with no expression, no feeling. I couldn't help it, somehow the capacity of feeling wasn't allowed me any more.

I walked from Middlefield on towards my house. It wasn't walking distance, but I walked, without even deciding whether to take the TTC or not.

I was seventeen — almost. But this wasn't fair. Seventeen is young. I didn't feel like having a baby right now!

Hot tears were rolling down my cheeks while I walked down the crowded path.

It's all right, Shabana, I told myself, you can cry, it's allowed as long as you don't allow crying to interfere with or decrease your strength. Cry a lot if you feel so, think of it as a sensation, these tears will dry, they won't control you, because you'll still be strong. Think of crying as a luxury.

My parents — what about my parents. What would they think, what did they expect — not this. I didn't want to face them. It was like I'd have to set up a presentation for them. Impress them by expressing how mature I would be about this. I would have to respond to all of their concerns and keep proving whatever I say over and over again. Just don't make them one of your problems, take them as strength if they will allow you. That's all I could tell myself.

My mind was stuck with the thoughts, and pictures of my Amma and Abbu as they were engraved into my mind. I tried to think of how I could get strength from them, but I couldn't. Too much was happening too fast.

Well, no homegirl could help me now. I needed higher guidance, strength, calm.

I was finally across the street from my house but was not ready to go in yet. I sat down on the bench in the park down the street. The weather is nice, I thought to myself. I saw the white mass of snow all around me and vaguely heard a few birds chirping. I guess when you first think of winter, you get depressed. It is like a monster that limits your life. You can't go out too much, it's so cold, and it gets dark too soon. It's just so gloomy. But when you sit and take a moment to look at the snow, it is sensationally beautiful. Babies are beautiful too ... they are lovely.

I felt weird as some type of a pleasant feeling filled my body and mind. It really was weird, how this happy feeling enveloped my thoughts, just like my feeling of shock did.

Babies are beautiful. They are possessive of you, and you can be possessive of your baby too and love them to the extreme, and you won't get hurt. Babies must love you more if you are all by yourself. I told myself all this to calm me.

I would soon have a big tummy. I saw myself wearing one of those big *shalwar kurtas* with the gorgeous embroidery like my Amma has. I would get all kinds of different coloured *kurtas*, and buttons with mirrors on them. I was finding things to feel happy about. I was accepting this baby — my baby, it would give me strength — I hoped....

This feeling of somewhat joy felt like it would last. So, I got up off the bench, walked to my house. No one was home yet; they would probably be home in no less than an hour.

I took off my jacket. The phone rang. It was Kurts, my boyfriend.

"Yo, Shabana — what's up?"

"Hi Kurts, how're you feelin'?"

I drifted off into another thought. This one began to cause panic in my head again. Kurts — wow, he had something to do with this baby too! He was what people will say the father of my baby! That was right, but what good would he do? Give me strength? Commitment? I mean it's like that is too much to ask! But I had a feeling he couldn't do it. I knew I needed all the strength and support I could get.

"Shabana, sorry I didn't call for so long but I — "

"Kurts, I got to talk to you."

"Yeah, man ..."

"Can you meet me outside my house in the evening? And don't cancel or we won't ever talk again." I hung up.

That was pretty cold, Shabana, I said to myself.

My parents got home. Oh it was hard to tell them something so personal. I didn't know how to start. If only I didn't have to look at their faces when I started with "I'm pregnant." I didn't have that much guts! This sentence had been bouncing with excitement all over inside me. It was dying to get out. I was afraid even to open my mouth, it might just jump out and arrive to the ears of my Amma and Abbu.

I was losing my appetite!

"I don't feel like eating, Amma."

"Janu, you sure?"

"I just got a funny feeling in my stomach."

"Well that's OK, remember to eat later. Can you tell Abbu it's time to eat?"

I went upstairs and came down with him. God, I couldn't look at my father, he always looked like he knew exactly what I was thinking, or if I was lying, or hiding something.

Calm down Shabana, remember your parents are probably the only people who care about you extremely, and can give you the most support. In the end, they are the ones who will make sure you survive.

Yeah, in the end.... No man, it was too hard.

I'd been waiting for Kurts, it had been a few minutes now.

"Shabana, what's up!"

"I'm cool."

"So what've you been up to?"

"Thinkin' about something we'd been up to."

Kurts and I walked on to the path from my house towards Ellesmere.

"Look, straight out. I'm pregnant. I'm not expectin' nothin' from you, so don't feel like you have to do me any favours." That's great, I just put him down. I just simply told him I thought he wouldn't give any support or show any concern, that I didn't even think he would ever be any help.

"Oh shit," Kurts slowly replied.

"I don't know what kind of feelings you have about this, but I really wanna know whether you have the strength to play a positive role in this situation. I wanna know what kind of role you're going to play."

"Have you told your parents?"

"Not yet. I needed to know your reaction to begin with."

"Man, I ain't ready for this."

"You're not ready for —"

"But, I know I should be a part of this, and I don't wanna be a problem."

Hm, the guy had brains! More sense than I expected, at least he thought he might become a problem for me, I mean, I really thought he could give me stress instead of support.

"I'll help you in whichever way you need."

That's right, I will help you, whichever way you need. What?! He didn't know what needs I would have? He didn't know nothin' man! It was too sad he didn't know.

"Do you know how you're going to help?"

"I ... I don't know ... how —"

How? I almost screamed out. Forget it, it wasn't worth askin' him. He couldn't conceive the idea of him helping, he just didn't know.

"Well that's kind of you. I'll catch you later."

"Hey, Shabana ... wait ..."

"We can talk about this another time if you want," I replied in my nice and polite style, which I use just when I know I am about to explode with anger.

"You sure —"

"Yeah, later."

One down, parents to go, I thought to myself. While I was walking back home, a car went by and I heard music from inside the car. It was Bob Marley. Positive vibration — the word positive — Bob Marley used it a lot. I thought being positive led you to being peaceful. But what is peace? The atmosphere of course — the view, scenery ... sanctuary! But that was like askin' for heaven while you're on earth. So what does peace really mean? Joy, joyous thoughts and feelings ... Which is achieved by positivity, positive thinking ... I'd never make it through with this baby for too long unless I was happy with myself. If I was depressed, my baby was sure to be depressed too; I had to keep my baby happy. So ... happy is positive and positive is the lane to peace. Peace between my parents and me, my baby and me, and everything else.

I felt like I could talk to my parents now. But not quite now ... tomorrow, when I was rested and feeling fresh.

At noon when I awoke everybody was in the basement watching TV, so I went upstairs and put on some music. I put on Tracey Chapman. Man, this woman was too much, everything she sang was heavy and realistic. "All that you have is your soul" and "careful of my heart": I loved those lines in her songs. She said you had to leave some love for yourself, at least enough to survive through whatever came your way. Yeah, like this baby! As I laughed inside, I questioned why I'd been thinking about this baby like it was some event I definitely wasn't looking forward to. The baby had done nothing, it wasn't to blame. Mistakes and misjudgements came into play on my part and on Kurts' part. We didn't know such a thing as responsibility! Plainly — it was carelessness. So why was it all dumped on me. Why, when the man is to blame just as much as the woman? If anybody tried to tell me otherwise, I'd know it was pure bullshit. I swear I'd kick their ass till they understood it clearly.

I was gettin' really upset now, finally anger had taken hold of me. We slipped together, we were irresponsible together. Then why was it that I alone had to make decisions around giving birth to babies. Or not. My heart was stunned, at the thought ...

Oh, I couldn't believe it had been only twenty days since I found out I was pregnant, yet I couldn't believe I still hadn't told my parents! But I wanted to; it was really burdening me that there was something so important that I had not even discussed with them. I had practically lost my appetite, I had big black bags under my tired eyes just because I couldn't keep a secret. Not one like this.

My mother walked past me with a cup of tea while I stared at her from the couch.

"Amma," I said, "Amma," I said. Amma, I whispered, I mumbled. Oh but my voice really did not come out. Blood raced fumingly in my body. Inside I cried as loud as I could: Amma, oh, Amma, why can't you feel that I am at the edge of destruction now? Can't you feel that I am about to fall off? Why don't you save me? Why is it so hard? Why? I am becoming so naïve and weak, I wish that you would just hug me.

"Amma," my voice churned out!

"*Jee*, Janu?" She was closer.

"Amma, I need to talk to you —" I got up.

She was on her way to do something or the other. She changed her mind and came over to me instead.

"What is it?" She sat herself down in front of me.

"It's — it's —"

"Yes, baby?"

"Yes, yes. Baby."

"Is everything okay?"

"Oh, Amma ..." I went over and sat beside her, shivering.

"What is it?"

"After I finish talking, and before you want to say something, please think about being sensitive because your support is essential. It isn't a joke. You know that I have had a relationship for six months now, with Kurts. You allowed me to go out with him, or anyone, because you trust my judgement, and you trust me to be sensible. Therefore whatever I do, I will be responsible for it, and excuses will not help. I will suffer my own consequences. I know what I have done, I know what I have to do. I am pregnant. I am going to take more responsibility for this than even my partner — but I wouldn't mind some support...."

"Yes, Janu. Tell me what it is."

My whole speech had stayed on my tongue. Oh no.

"Fear nothing, Shabana. Say what you need to say."

"I am pregnant," I screamed like a whisper. I looked straight at her face.

She seemed as if she hadn't heard it still. She wasn't looking at me, but through me, straight through the present into the future! After about five minutes of silently slurping the tea, she spoke, "What do you think of abortion?"

I didn't even think of abortion! Abortion ... What a relief, I could live my own life as freely as I wanted. Nothing would get in my way if I had an abortion, and I deserved it. This wasn't planned, I didn't even know if I would be able to get through this or not. You have to have a baby when you are ready and have time for it. You have to be capable of seriously bringing up the baby. I wasn't old enough. And it was a joke that I thought I would actually be able to get through this!

"I didn't think of abortion...." I was completely dumbfounded and didn't even hear myself speak.

"Well what did you think about? About raising the baby, while you are so young, at the age when this much pressure, stress can break you? Because it's a lot of work and money and no one else can do this for you! It is not fair on you...."

We talked for the longest time.

I heard silence. I felt silence.

I thought about my baby the whole week. I skipped almost all my classes doing it. Finally, I went over to Kurts' and let him comment on what I had to say.

"What do you think of abortion?" I asked innocently,

although I knew he would make me feel anything but that.

"What? You're going to have an abortion? No way, man."

"Yeah? I heard, and I feel the truth of it, that if it is my body that will develop the baby and it is my person who is going to bring her up, I think it should be my choice, clearly."

"That's killing a baby!!" He was already accusing me.

"Well tell me this, Kurts! What are you gong to do for the baby? How are you going to take responsibility? Are you even going to take any responsibility?!" I blurted these words out with a feeling of distastefulness.

"I don't know ! I mean, I'm not sure, I don't know what to do. How could I help you? I got plans to go to —"

"So what the fuck gave you the right to tell me I'd be murdering a baby? Tell me? You're just an ignorant bastard — you can't be pregnant for me! You won't have to carry the kind of stress I will! Tell me?! How can you accuse me of murdering? Why don't I count? WHY DON'T I COUNT??? Don't you think a baby would take a lot away from me too? You have no fuckin' idea how much I would need to give up here." I wanted to scream so loud so that I would break the surface of the earth.

"I —"

"So don't give me any bullshit; no guilt," I cut him off, and sternly walked away.

I was done with Kurts, no hope for him — no hope for me and him.

I'm in labour ... feels OK, it's goin' smoother then I ever imagined, it's — Holy shit!!! Scream, scream, Shabana! Scream for your life!! I thought I was supposed to get some drugs for this pain! Who the fuck does this doctor think he is? Not giving me any drugs! I want something to kill this pain — Holy shit! Amma says it's like eating fresh strawberries and green chillies. Why the hell can't I just eat the strawberries, god dammit, we have to eat the green chillies too!!! Breath in and out. Strawberries and chillies. Strawberries and chillies, that's what you're feeling, Shabana, stay cool. NO! I want a pain killer — now! Where is my mother?? I want someone, someone who cares for me, someone who will care for me forever, and I want them now. I need someone now! I don't taste any strawberries any more, they're all chillies. I feel burning inside me!! I wanna know what the fuck is the joy of labour, I wanna know what's the joy of natural birth! These are the Nineties and I want my pain killers!!!

My face all flushed, red, as they put the baby in my lap. Just the sight of this baby is breathtaking. Feet like rose petals, eyes like sunlight, hands seeking love. I hold my breath — tears once again drip onto my face, they don't ask for permission or anything, they just barge in.... I still hold my breath and as I am forced to breathe in again, I begin to cry loudly. My tears are hot. I feel my mouth moving, saying ... I can relax: at last.

Relax, there is somebody who will care for you now. Forever.

My baby is lovely.

Well, I cannot always do "the sensible thing."

FAUZIA RAFIQ

Saheban & the Crisis of Identity

PART 1

From The Adventures of Saheban: A Biography of the Relentless Warrior

Not a continuous account of her life, the following pages are an independent narration of one of Saheban's major wars waged in the olden times of 3000s. Like millions of other women on earth, this author also is fascinated by this great woman warrior of her time.

BORN IN THE MILKEN State of Pacpenistan[1], Saheban's earliest war was waged against the crisis of identity that surrounded her at the time of her birth.

Over the years, there has been an incredible amount of speculation around her "strange behaviour" as a newborn baby. And, indeed, this "strangeness" has been offered as proof of her ostensible "urge" to commit violence against men, an allegation perpetually levelled against her by most learned male historians. Yes, you are right, we are talking about the incident where immediately after her birth Saheban scratched the face of the doctor, who happened to be a male.[2]

The fact of the matter is what follows:

Saheban's identity was put in crisis by the Keepers of the Pure Penisoids (hitherto called KOPPs) when she was in the process of becoming a fetus. The KOPPs, with the characteristic cunning of a colourless enemy, had colonized the brain of Jattee, Saheban's mother.[3] The colonizers took over the central communication support systems, sending viruses in her think tank. Resultantly, the inner voice of Jattee, whenever spoke to Saheban in the womb, called her "my son." Her mother's inner voice was elated, loving and in awe of Saheban (who her mother assumed was a He, and so objective situationally, Saheban also assumed herself to be a He). This sense of perpetual comfortability available to male fetuses or assumed male fetuses is very relaxing for the fetus. Saheban was physically strong, developed high self-esteem and felt comfortable with her body in the womb of her mother.

When she came out of the womb, however, the situation changed with some drastic implications and an uncontrollable speed. Saheban came out eager to see her mother's face. She needed to concretize the loving, elating and in-awe-of-her/him voice.

She found her mother in split second from among many. She willed the woman who was holding her to take her to her mother. Her mother, instead of looking at her face, went for her warm covering cloth.

Okay, maybe she wants to see my body first, like I wanted to see her face first. People have the right to be different. Why get alarmed?

Her mother glanced between Saheban's legs.

What is she looking at? Saheban wondered and that's when she heard her mother wail in such pain that she could not help but jump into a state of shock, directly from her peacefully floating state of wonderment.

"What is it?" She screamed the question at her mother.

"You don't have it." her mother wailed, strangling million tears.

"What? What is it that I don't have, Amma?" she screamed louder, now almost in panic.

"The thing between your legs, you fool." Her mother was getting hysterical.

"The thing between my legs?" She wriggled and came right back into the comfortable fetal position. Her head snugly fit between her two knees, she had an excellent and clear view of between-her-legs. She looked intensely. There indeed was something between her legs. Mother did not look closely, Saheban thought with a sigh of relief.

"It is here," she said comfortingly to her wailing mother. "It is here, Amma, it is."

Her mother did not acknowledge.

"Amma, it's here, Amma," she shouted as loud as she physically could.

Her mother felt so mad at her that she broke the continuity and rhythm of her wailing and said to her.

"That's not IT."

"What's not it?"

"That."

"But it is between the legs."

"Yes, I know. I have that too."

"Then why do you say that it's not it?"

"It's not. You have THAT."

"I have what?"

"That."

"That?"

"Yeah, that."

"What's that?"

"It's definitely not IT."

"Yeah, well I already got that."

"What have you got?"

"I got something between my legs but it's not IT, it's THAT."

"Yeah, you got that."

"Okay, so now, what's that?"

"It's not —"

"Yeah, yeah, I have that, what I have is not IT but that, so what's THAT?"

"That's not —"

"I got that, Amma. Now listen to me carefully, do not get anxious, just listen to me."

"Okay."

"What is IT?"

"It's not —"

"No, Amma. What — is — IT's — name? What do you call it?"

"P-pee-nus-s."

"Pee-nuss?"

"Yeah."

"Now, Amma, what — is — THAT's — name? What do you call that?"

"*Andam-e-Nihani*, dammit."

"Sorry?"

"*Andam* — don't make me say that again, dammit, it's bad enough as it is."

"But I didn't get it."

"Yeah, you didn't." Her mother sighed and cried.

"And it's not pee-nuss?"

"No."

"And everyone is supposed to have IT?"

"Yeah."

"So, where is my pee-nuss?" she demanded to know.

"You don't have one."

"Why not?"

"Get away from me." Her mother was now absolutely disgusted with her.

"Don't close the inner communication system, Amma!"

Jattee turned her face away.

"Amma! Don't do that to me."

Jattee was now wailing for everyone to hear.

She closed the channels, Saheban thought, and just for something that I forgot to bring with me? Something called pee-nuss which is between the legs. Oh, my god! It must be important. It can still be in her womb. Where is the midwife, she can get it out. I must try to get it back, Amma is going nuts.

As chance would have it, just at that moment when Saheban faced a short term crisis situation at ten minutes of age, the doctor picked her up.

"Where is my pee-nuss?" she screamed at the doctor.

The doctor had never bonded with her so he didn't get it. He thought she was screaming and crying for no reason at all.

"Where is my pee-nuss?" She tried to communicate again.

The doctor paid no attention to her whatsoever.

"Where is my pee-nuss?" She felt tremendous sense of oppression and a breach of her rights by this obvious silencing and forced invisibility.

So, she had to fight it. And in her struggle to gain a voice and to preserve her right to be heard, she chose to do the only thing she could do under her circumstantial limitations. She went and scratched his clean shaven cheeks with her ten tiny soft nails.

The doctor who had IT between his legs instead of THAT also had an extremely fragile ego. It is obvious that he could not put Saheban out of his mind, ever, and so instantly came out with this sob story when Saheban was gaining media attention for her war against the Thick Grey Waters.[4]

After that there were small exploits but a major gain came when she was three and a half. Like everyone else, Saheban was also required to study Wholly KOPPs. Her teacher was an elderly bearded priest always wearing white cotton clothes to add emphasis to his purity and holiness. While teaching her he would pick her up and put her in his lap where she often felt something hard underneath her. The holy man would rock her on the surface of the hard thing to bring in unison the rhythm as he reverently recited verses, often going into a powerful fit of religio-spiritual ecstasy.

Every day Saheban wondered about the hard thing that she was continually being rocked on, feeling a sense of acute intimidation by the fit every now and then. One day, the priest was busy rocking her when something clicked into place within Saheban's cognition and discovery process. It seemed to her she might have found an answer to her queries. She slid down from his lap without letting the hard thing move away, then before she picked her bum up she reached under her and clutched it firmly.

"Is this IT?" she asked eagerly.

The holy man ogled his eyeballs and screamed.

"Is this IT?" She wanted an answer for sure.

The holy man tried to get up.

She refused to let go.

The holy man screamed again and then jerked himself away from her grip, screamed again and then scrambled out of his own room used as a school for young children.

Needless to say, Saheban was truly taken aback at this turn of events.

She went home and found her mother working in the kitchen.

"Amma, I got a hold on IT."

"Got a hold on what?"

"IT."

"You did what?"

"Got a hold on IT."

"O'my God! Whose IT was it?"

"Maulvi-Jee's."

Her mother fainted holding an antique china serving bowl in her hand.

The consequence of this was multi-faceted at best. Jattee lost her job, becoming a homeless single mother; Saheban's father stayed on and was promoted to the position of pimp from the lowly wage of a sentry.

Many attribute these developments to the incredible loss of the bowl but in-depth research clearly brings other factors to light.

It is now proven that the following interaction between the Master, Maulvi-Jee and Saheban's father did take place the same day, right after the bowl was broken.

Master: Yes, Maulvi? Why are you here wasting my time?

Maulvi: Master, I have important business.

Master: I am not in the mood for transcendental quirks, you understand?

Maulvi: Yes, Master.

Master: Go on and wrap it up fast.

Maulvi: It is complicated....
Master: Wrap it up, you son of a dog.
Maulvi: Yes, Master. S-Saheban has the spirit of Satan incarnate....
Master: Oh, interesting. Who is Saheban?
Maulvi: The daughter of your sentry, me Lord.
Master: Oh, very interesting. I wasn't aware he had daughters....
Maulvi: I beg forgiveness for interrupting you.
Master: You do it at your own risk, you son of an unnamed father.
Maulvi: Thank you, Master. Saheban is only about four, me Lord.
Master: Very disappointing. *"Kaun jeeta hai teri zulf ke sur ho ne tuk."*
Maulvi: Master, we may not judge her according to her age. She is evil, Satan incarnate.... *La haul Valla....*
Master: What did she do?
Maulvi: [Brings his voice really low. Allah Baksh the oral historian says that this part of the conversation was not heard by the ear-witness.]
Master: Incredible. Call her father.
Maulvi: [Tells the ear-witness to bring Saheban's father.]
Father: Master ...
Master: You have two options: you throw your female shit out of my house or ...
Father: I will do it, Master.
Master: Excellent. Good boy. Sit.
Father: Thank you, Master.
Master: You are promoted from my sentry to my pimp.
Father: They will leave before sundown, Master.
Master: Now bring something young and juicy. But not too young.

Father: Long live the Master.
Ear-witness: Down with the evil.
Maulvi: Down with the female spirit of Satan.

It is clear from the above account that Saheban and her mother were made homeless by a total misrepresentation of facts and that the bowl was not even once mentioned as a factor in it. Also, the myth about Saheban being the "female spirit of Satan" apparently comes from this same interaction.

[Part 1 ends here]

Endnotes

1. Historians give conflicting accounts of the origin and meaning of this name. The literal meaning of the term is "The Milken State of Pure Penises" and is used to mean "The Milken Land of the People with Pure Penises." The concept of the purity of the penis, historians believe, comes from the fact that the majority of penesoids living in this land choose to remove the outer skin of the head of the penis, thus making it pure. The word "Milken" refers to the breasts of a woman in a perpetual post-natal situation, and so is taken as an indication of gender equality.

The progressive school of male historians and linguists differ with the above interpretation. They trace the origin of the name from the word "pack" believing that the name means "The Land of Packed Penises," while the League of Women Historians rejects it, knowing it to be a "grave and misleading understatement of the actual state of penises at this time in Pacpenistan." The League argues that the term simply means "The Land of a Pack of Penises" (as in the "pack of wolves").

2. The practice of hiring male midwives was strongly opposed by the World Midwivery Organization, a subsidiary of The United Midwives of the Mother Earth, on account that this practice was a conspiracy to take women's jobs and pregnant women's rights away. This view was militantly opposed by the World Congress of Totally Unreal Women Against Women (WCTUWAW). (The

name was later abbreviated to WAW. A spokesperson of the WAW, Major Generally Dolly Civic, in her opening address to the 129th congress of her organization said, "We might be known by as many names as our independent and wealthy chapters worldwide, including of course our coloured, ignorant but privileged sisters in the Twenty-fifth World. But what explains our mandate best in three letters is the word WAW. Translate it into your own languages, my unreals, and have no fear because our brothers around the world approve of it. As a proof of this assertion, I present the E-mail received moments ago right here in our head offices in Saudi Arabia, a message sent by the order of Totally Unreal Men supporting the promotion of WAW as our motto." Just for the record, the establishment of head office in Saudi Arabia was symbolic in nature while this international organization was guided by its regional office in the state of Florida in North America.)

3. It might be of interest to our readers that Jattee was honoured by the Great Undergound Womb Organization (GUWO) with the title "Womb Defender 10" in the early 1980s.

4. For her war against the Thick Grey Waters, please refer to page number 227,800 in the unabridged version of *Adventures of Saheban: A Biography of the Relentless Warrior* available at your local women's bookstore, under the counter, of course.

Just So I Can Walk

Once i found
a foot-long butterfly
dead
under my shoe
(my foot was in it)
i froze, by the side of the road
where i stood
admiring the spring streets of Manila 1981
my heart
sank

taking my memory
with it
at that moment
a girl, child
lost
in the jungle
of men (characteristic: vulture-power)
and women,
panic-struck
danger-surrounded, shrieked
with all her might
a few feet
away
from where i stood
cold
in the summer valley of Himalayas 1969

head-crazed, flesh-torn
i entered
the war zone
looking
for the girl, child
lost
in the jungle of men
and women (characteristic: snake-poison)
and at that moment
i stumbled upon
hundreds of fish
dead
floating belly up
in the autumn Lake of Ontario 1993
vulture-power cutting the air
snake-poison slithering in water

woman-memory (characteristic: womb-protection)
buried deep
inside the skull
unshed tears
gathering heat
heat, burn
burning
desire

hands trembling with fear
scoop
the butterfly
legs melting beneath me
stand
yes, beside
the girl, child
hashish-lungs filter the poison
from the domain
of waterlings

just so i can
walk
the streets of Manila
valleys of Himalayas
the beaches of Toronto

ZARA SULEMAN

The Curve

smooth and silky the line draws
close to your body then far away
inside lines hugging turns
that feel so warm
against my
hands

the sloping sensual circular
motions of my tongue along
your flesh, tasting your
skin inhaling your
sweet seductive
smell through
my body

my fingertips leaving
prints into your tissue
lawyers wanting to connect
with your body as one, hands

melting into your waist and hips
heat from a fire, from your fire
pull me in, look up,
we meet
eye to eye

the curve, the line of your
fleshy flesh pulling over your
body, from under your arms to
your tummy, the curve runs
its course, guiding my hands
all over then aligning to the
curve, holding tightly and softly
kissing, licking, teasing the curve
wanting to please
every curve, wanting to conform
to every curve,
wanting every curve
of yours next to
mine.

Kitch & Talk

Four generations
of women sitting in the
kitchen
the smells of cumin,
mustard seeds, onions,
turmeric, and saffron
simmer in the background

the cosy feeling of
warmth rises from
the hot cups of tea
before them
they are talking about
how it used to be
how it was, and
what would happen?
In my day says
one woman in Kuchi
when we were young
says one woman in Gujarati
my daughter doesn't
understand, says one
woman in Urdu
I do understand says
the woman in English
blends of spices and scents
flavours in the air mix
with ages of conversation
poetic almost,
memorable moments,
forgotten times,
thoughtful comments,
hopeful futures.

SMITA VIR TYAGI

Two Love Poems

I

Sounds of domesticity
waft through the house
in tandem
with the sun,
orchestrating each morning
with familiar regularity.

The *dudhwala* is clattering
at the door with his large aluminum canisters.
Meena Bai watches him complaining
the price is too high, the milk is watery.
The city buffaloes aren't so healthy it seems.
The *pauwalla* is ringing his bicycle bell
Pav? Pav? and is waved away.
All the world's astir.

Eyes meet
over rims of cups
vapours of freshly brewed tea
drift lazily between us
enjoin
our lives again
as we begin another day
together.

II

firm walled chest
pressed into her back
face fanning her nape,
stray hair lightly rising
to the rhythm of breath.
solid,
gentle on her chest;
a length of leg curved beside hers

thigh to thigh, knee to knee
foot curled into smaller foot,
two "S"s snuggled into shape
deeply restful,
quiet, unmoving,
crisp, crimped sheet
telling the story of sleep.

SMITA VIR TYAGI

On First Love and Feminism at 16

Sun rays in a crack
of a half-opened door
your love edged past its half-resistance
tiptoeing from behind
holding me captive, unawares.
In your wide, firm embrace
diffused, translucent
I radiated your light.
Slashed about,
played, danced even
like weightless particles in the air
bathed in delight.

Held powerless
to gravitate towards my own suns
I stayed
encircled within your radii
unconscious
that somewhere in the pull and push
of our interplay
orbited the footprints
of an unknown singularity,
the real me.

I might have scattered my being thus
fading star, shower of sparks
sharp points of light
lost quickly beyond the pale.
Great gusts of passing winds
gathered the particles of my dispersed self

and flew them,
across bright galaxies, limitless skies
limitless skies,
into the palm of a new universe ...
Now,
my feet are poised
on the curvature pointing to infinity.

I am afraid ...

I taste the salt on my forehead
dismayed, and think
It's not this toil I want
as beads on my brow
guts parched, thirsts drying
over the incessant heat of the stove,
I am afraid my soul may perish
unsung, on this clean and shining floor
disappear into oblivion
even as I watch it go.

My mind turns to order
like the rooms I tidy in the day
no more panning the horizon
in creative disarray. I retract
from my reflection in the polished
kitchen sink, sudden reminder of a
secret self, forgotten notebooks,
the scratch of pen and ink.

I'm afraid of virtue, sacrifice, noble gains
raising a fine family, gifting my youth
to this exalted capacity, unstoppable
machinations of living, endless tasks,
mindless circularity.
Out of a sense of duty, I begin
to lose my mind.

I am afraid
I am enveloped
by the personae I must be
all the while my heart cries
"This isn't me, this isn't me!"
I am terrified
I have no impetus, though it appears
I have a choice.
Certified "Good daughter-in-law"
or
mad housewife.

VINITA SRIVASTAVA

Grappling

VINITA SRIVASTAVA SLOWLY sank underground. As she sank, her eyes slipped to the sign denoting the subway station. Occupying her mind with only tangible visuals, she noncommittally noticed long winter coats and walking stereos on their way to work.

Subway signs look like tombstone markings.

Court today. Fourth bloody day.

Another sleepless night. (What would help — to spend it with you?)

Another sleepless night. Explanations don't expand from my tongue. I am alone on a busy street. So many kisses and extended arms. If I were more alone would I want them? I am a submarine. Armoured. Trapped in a smaller world. I am a caged animal, let out only to jump through fired hoops at the circus. Trained, fed and stalked.

There is a delay at the Doncaster subway. I should have walked. Vinita fixed her eyes on the large yellow and black poster in front of her. Join the fast track through courses at George Brown College. Join the fast track. Join the fast track. Join the fast track. George Brown College. Join the fast track. At least a five minute delay they announce. Mob mentality last time the subway went out. I wish everybody had decided to throw out temporality. Spirituality sit. Instead it looked like Chicken Little was right. (The sky was falling.) People running by — angry that you too are not in a rush. Storming off to life-saving-boardroom-shelters. Join the fast track. I'll be late. Join the fast track....

This courthouse was once beautiful. Now, holes in the stairs, uneven marble, and smokers everywhere. So what if I was two hours late yesterday? Not as if they needed me to testify until today. No need for them to put an APB on me. Vinita approached Mr. Looks-like-Michael-moustache.

"Where were you? We were supposed to start at seven o'clock this morning!"

Cop humour. Vinita smiled for him.

More people here today. Odd group. There's my bench. Empty. Mr. Moustache stands as usual. Strange how that worked. Those not remotely belonging to the judicial system sit, those who do, stand. Strange how it also splits up men and women. Pretty soon I'll be surrounded by suit legs, and pipes and cigarettes. Vinita takes a seat on the very hard bench outside courtroom number 126 in front of the "No Smoking, Maximum Fine $1000.00" sign.

Yes, officer, I'd like to report three lawyers breaking the law on the second floor of Old City Hall.

Yes, all smoking. Yes, all male. Yes, all arrogant.

What's wrong. WRONG. What's wrong?

Yes, I'd like to report something strange going on in my street. Another battle. Fist on fist. Scream. Inside I am grow-ing, swelling, bursting, running through orange stomachs, hoping for a nice blue instead. The orange liquid concrete in my stomach and my shoulders slowly solidifies. I have been thrown into a small blue pool. All four corners are visible. Then, as the concrete sinks, not at all.

The two young men in the odd group outside the courtroom harmonize to occupy themselves.

I write the songs that make the whole world sing.

Wonder why everyone thinks they're here on drug charges? Vinita slowly swallowed the small group to her left. An old woman in a grey coat and slippers, three young women in pantsuits and high heels, and two long-haired young men in jeans. Together, a family. How can I file for divorce, Mama? the young woman asks.

Amazing Grace

How Sweet the Sound

What do you want a divorce for?

Steve. Vinita maintained her façade of reading her book as she waited to learn more.

Hush little baby don't say a word

He's dead, you don't have to divorce a dead man. You're a widow.

Vinita smiled. Getting up to relieve the wooden bench, Vinita strained to see inside number 126.

Look! There.

The glass window on the door to the courtroom. Feels like I'm looking through Him's glasses. The egg-eyed sergeant arrived bearing coffee. The four police officers, and the custodian/witness enveloped the sergeant. Vinita remained fixed, unsure. The janitor was still upset that he went outside in the cold to smoke, while the lawyers stayed warm.

Have some coffee, Vinita, the sergeant prescribed. But not too much or you'll be in the bathroom all afternoon. At least that's what coffee does to me, the sergeant chuckled, looking up for approval. After the cream and sugar, the police officer lived on the Toronto's Daily Tabloid.

Police officers ogling sunshine girls. I can't hide my disapproval any more. It's too obvious. Chicken wings and beer and degrading woman jokes. Night out on the town. Damn.

Noticing Vinita's alienation from the group of men, the officers offered her the golden boy.

No thanks. (Small black-and-white versus full colour page.)

I don't read that OTHER paper. They're biased against us, one of the officers justified to Vinita. Oh. What about the other one? There ARE three. (Vinita clenched to casually continue.)

Look, the sergeant glared, that's not the immigration truck that comes in here every morning. It's a truck full of city criminals coming to court. And they think we're racist. Can't help if there are more black criminals in this city.

Living in this city we are told that we are wonderfully multicultural. But I know this society of multi-cultures as one culture of vultures circle above us looking for rotting meat.

Beat the rap man! A black youth shouts to the black un-uniformed police officer sitting next to the Mr. Moustache on the bench outside the courtroom.

You'll be next, Vini-TTa, a sergeant warns, make sure you're not chewing any gum or they'll make you stick it on the end of your nose! The sergeant shakes his head, marvelling at his own humour.

Vinita Sree-vis-ta-va, a court guard announces, struggling with the name, causing the courtroom waiters to look up at Vinita getting up from her wooden bench. Vinita stretches into court number 126. A black gown with red trimming envelopes the white judge. Eagle face. Heard she's turned MAN. Mahogany everything. Kermit the Frog green. White faces. Large old windows, beautiful, but ruined by the heating radiators underneath them. A large viewing gallery.

All rise.

I thought they only did that in movies.

The defendant makes a show of trying to rise out of his wheelchair. Asshole. He didn't need a wheelchair four months ago.

Hold the Bible in your right hand and swear.

Shit. Funny. Just listen to the man. Hindu by birth, non-religious by choice. My anger swells. I wonder if they have a copy of the Koran, or the Bhagavadgita, or the Torah, or any other sacred documents besides the Bible? Aren't they supposed to offer us a choice?

Without too much apparent hesitation, Vinita picked up the pocked Bible on her right.

Do you promise to tell the whole truth and nothing but the truth?

NO!? How would they know if someone was lying? I thought all witnesses got some sort of chair. Even if it is a hard wooden one. But remain standing and uncomfortable please. Mr. Young Moustache told me to be extra polite to Mr. Weasel. Defence hates it when you answer their weasely questions politely.

Spell your full name please.

V-I-N-I-T-A. S as in Sam, R-I, V as in Victor, A-S ...

Next?!

Recount. Srivas-T-A-V-A.

Miss Ser-Vis-Tah; is that the correct pronunciation? The defence lawyer smiled as he looked directly at Vinita.

Uh no, but don't worry about it. Vinita looked down slightly.

The defence lawyer gave a large smile.

O! But we must.

All right, if the weasel insists (let's make him speak Hindi). The correct pronunciation is Vinita Shrrevastahvah. Vinita pronounced with extreme rapidity.

Miss Sree vaas ta va? The defence attorney politely asked. Knew I'd get him. No victory.

No. Vinita smiled. Shrrevastahvah, Vinita calmly replied with her grade two teacher-like voice. Slower, anglicized, articulated.

He still mispronounced it. Small victories. Pretty shallow. Weasel. Trying to make friends. His smile looks phony.

Do NOT return that smile. My tiny battles are turned big by new hatreds, useless victories. Why am I here?

Vinita, can you tell us what happened to you on the night of December 8, 1988 at approximately 9:04 pm?

Seems like they already know what happened. Why am I here? They will not make me cry.

In detail? Vinita looked up for support towards the crown attorney, who offered none. Felt like I was being followed as soon as I left the subway.

A woman talked into a Darth Vadar mask. Or maybe it's more like an airplane oxygen mask. It looks smelly. For the record. A very small moustached man sits directly to her right. He is holding a small paperback. Probably Plato. What's he doing here?

What time exactly did you arrive on the subway platform?

EXACTLYYYYY? Who knows EXACTLY what time it is ever? It did TOO happen.

How many seconds were you on the platform before you noticed another man?

One Mississippi, two Mississippi. I don't know. Shut up.

When you first looked up, how far away was he?

Think. Wish I could close my eyes. I am afraid, was afraid. Ten feet, ten yards? Ten metres?

You've indicated that the platform was empty when he first yelled. And to be fair to you, I have used your word "yell." Would you say that if other people were there on the platform they would have heard this "yell"?

Indicated. Said. Justice. Vantage points. I can't get another. I only know what I heard, I can't give you any information about someone else's vantage point. Vinita answered somewhat facetiously. The School of Philosophy, thank you Socrates for your arrogance.

Describe your attacker.

My memory shuts off. Look. I said look. Come. I said come with me. I start with me in my red jacket. No. Later, at home, I am wearing the green. He wears a charcoal grey coat just past or above his knees. Stubble. White. Charcoal hair. Thin hair. Behind his ears. Mid-fifties. Hands holding knife.

Forget. Forget. NO. I said forget.

Describe his voice.

It was gruff. Vinita replied, after a pause, directly to the defence lawyer, avoiding her peripheral view of the man in the wheelchair to her left.

What was the tone and how deep was his voice?

Tone. Timbre. Weasel. I am fed up, and I don't care. He RAN four months ago. What's he doing in a wheelchair?

Do you sing? He was an alto, and definitely not a baritone.

Vinita smiled into a giggle.

Weasel. Not so serious any more. I still have concrete shoulders.

Back room watchers didn't think court was like this.

It is aggravatingly unclear.

Hands with knives and nicotine stains. Now, hands that turn the wheelchair. WHEELCHAIR.

I am an angry animal waiting to get out. I want to make him RUN now like he did before. RUN. Instead I jump through fire. I am trained. I am fed. I am stalked.

How big was his knife?

Confusion. The weasel smiles, noting the confusion on my face. Well, was it uh, six inches, twelve inches, one, ... or ... ah ... two ... inches thick? Surely you must have some idea? Vinita attempts to demonstrate with her two hands. But for the record, it must be said.

I am a locomotive labouring along. He must look so nice to those others, an elderly harmless man, with slicked hair, in a blue suit, in a wheelchair.

How was he holding the knife? Like this ... like this ... or maybe like this? The weasel moves his hands in yet another position.

Is there anything else you can tell me about his hands?

Think. Was it really like this? High. Yes. His hands are high in his chest.

You mean you didn't notice all the nicotine stains, the brown spots, all over his hands?

Silence, the court feels silent. You fool. Maybe his knife wasn't so big. Did I really see his hands? The crown attorney looks like she's given up.

The knife, not the hands. The hands do not matter. I saw the knife.

I wonder if years from now people will say to the weasel; Remember when you put that guy in that wheelchair? That was the most brilliant move of your defence career.

I fall backward in time to the beginning.

I am not yet eleven years old. I remember my mother, my busy, caring, wonderful mother. We are shopping together. Stainless steel pans. Plastic boxes. Books and Toys. Mittens. Every aisle that I go to so does the man behind me. I am scared.

WHAT IS HE DOING?

Suddenly aching to find my mother or my sister who I do find in the Books and Toys. So does the man behind me.

Determined to find my mother I grab my sister and, calm

and terrified, find shelter in the stainless steel with my unsuspecting mum.

I leap back to the present and realize that the face of the man in the wheelchair looks like the face of the man in the store.

I want to get rid of this man. Play judge. Why is killing someone a dream? I think about my drugstore psychology.

Yesterday a man on the bus stared and stared. The woman across from me looked up to him, looked down again.

HOLD your head up. I silently scream.

She is reduced to ashamed embarrassment. He followed her off the bus — I wanted to come between them — but he was quick. I wanted to trip him.

I walk out of courtroom number 126. Determined. I am too angry to cry. Hold. I said hold your head up.

The sergeant comes to shake my hand.

I leave the courthouse. People walk around me and through me. Just like the cold wind that travels into my body. The cold air enters my body and then becomes warm air, and I am aware of the warmth that my body radiates.

Then I spot the weasel.

I'm sorry I was so rough on you in there. But it's a job and somebody has to do it.

I say nothing to him. But I am filled with pride. Look, just look. He knows I have power.

I can see through to him. And he is shocked by my strength.

Like the stars grappling desperately for a space to be seen through the clouds, I burst into the space around me. Grappling. I am a resilient, reticent, glowing star.

My dance is quiet. Glorious. And I am power.

DHARINI ABEYESKERA

Tactics
(Sri Lanka, 1989)

Most evenings
there's a young woman
at the bus halt.
Flask of hot tea
and pillow in hand.
On her way to see someone in hospital.

One day
she's searched.
Posters in the pillow
paste in the flask.
Working for the cause
enemy of law and disorder
rife in our land.

Next day
she's but a thing on the roadside
burning in her pyre
an old tire.
People come gawk
pass by and don't talk.
Her comrades say:
"Hey it's do and die.
Hope she didn't croak."
The way things go
blood will flow.

Queen's Park on Labour Day's Eve
(September, 1990)

For many moons now
The circle forms
Come sun, come rain,
Come park security.

The sun shines through the trees
On lengths of red cloth.
The sounds of ripping rend the air
The pile grows of red arm bands
Blood bright
We will fight
For our birthright.

I conduct my own vigil
Silently.
What can I

A seeker of refuge in this land
Say?

An unexpected bonus
A circus next door ...

Free burgers, pop and T-shirts;
A war over tent rights
Pegs in! Pegs out!
Lost before it began.
A marching band
bright in blue with orange flags
right in the thick of a mob
hooting Peterson's bus.
High jinks!

Speeches, songs and they all go away.
No tents, no way they'll stay.

The circle is a long time forming
The wind grows colder
The mosquitoes bolder.

It's dark when I leave
A single question
Ricochetting in my brain
Whose permission did I seek
Before settling this land?

During the stand-off at Oka, a group of First Nations people camped at Toronto's Queen's Park legislature in support of the Mohawk Nation. David Peterson was the Ontario premier at the time.

From the Don Valley Parkway

Massive steel grids
Hold up the bridge
Which I with thousands of others
Cross everyday.

Mute testimony
To those that come before me.
Their sweat and blood
A sacrifice
On the altar of development.

FAWZIA AHMAD

The Battle

when will you get it?
we meet
we strategize
we cry
we scream
we are hysterical
we educate
we are tired
you hurt us
you stomp out
you call us
homophobic
classist
ableist
anti-Semitic
sizeist
why?
because
we said

you are racist
when will you get it?
we go to work
we look around
brown faces
only brown faces
white women are sick?
last night
you were kicking
and screaming
flinging papers
and so outraged
because we said
you are racist
today
you are all sick?
who is hurt by racism?
i may be mistaken
who goes to work
after the pain
who does all this
wonderful work?
why, we do
brown women
strong beautiful
brown women

Latifa

I love her
She was so beautiful
I couldn't resist
I looked after her
I spoiled her
Everyone admired her
She shielded me from
the cruel eyes of
the outside world
One day I left
She was sad
No one looked after her
She died inside
When I returned
I cried
I mourned
to see her suffering
It will never be the same
Next time I leave
would you please water
my plant Latifa?

TSHERING WANGMO DHOMPA

The Echoing Song

Indoctrination does not suit me
for I think I have fallen
deep into the habit
of touching rosaries and deities
in my sleep.
My heart wanders
constantly,
Abutting on longings
and indifference,
to run through endless meadows,
my legs lost in soft grass and dancing flowers, blue
  and red.
Blue
like the naked sky
caressing tall mountains and black tents of wandering
  nomads;

singing love songs
with the cold wind.
I could easily be the red-cheeked nomad girl
bending over yaks and sheep
reading the passion in the songs of the wind.
This obsession has spread
from the ubiquitous ears and eyes
to settle awkwardly in dreams.
I think the old nun,
with her prayer wheel and wrinkled smile
slips into the past,
in her dreams.
I ought to ask her,
if I could take her hand.
And forever walk
those endless green fields.

Translucent Dreams

I would have myself
shrink
to the size of a blue and green marble.
And be free,
content,
in a torn pocket of a little urchin.
Alone
or jostling
in and about ten others,
or roll
in blissful dust, headlong into my neighbours.
Or sleep.
Warm sleep.
In grubby hands
that hug me close.

FARZANA DOCTOR

Banu

My mother taught me to fight.
In the eleven short years I knew her
She taught me about justice.
  Racism.
  Love.

"You're a chocolate face."
"So what. You're a vanilla face."

I grew up in a small suburban white town.
I went to Brownies, said the Lord's Prayer,
Disliked Friday evening Gujarati classes and
Always wanted to fit in.

"Paki go home."

My mother swelled in fury
When her little girl repeated the ugly words

She had been told at school.
And so she went out to find justice.

Banu marched to Ed Broadbent's office
And spoke of her children.
And of racism and Pakis.
"And we are not from Pakistan."

Years after the cancer took over
Years after I tried to forget her
Years after I shunned the med-keeners who looked
   like me
Years after I streaked my hair blond
She returned to me.

And I remembered.

I remembered the name-calling
And how she got mad
And I remembered
How she went down fighting.

Did she know that on that day,
She planted a gem in her little girl's mind
Which many years after her death
Would grow
Inside my Indo-phobic
Multiculturized
Coconut head?

Did she know that her one act
Would help create a
Woman who would love herself

Her brown skin
Her dark eyes
The beauty of women?

If I could know her today
We would sit together
And have *chai*.
We would speak of our lives
Of truth
Of justice
And of "Pakis" who
Would not go home
But stayed to change the world.

SHANTI DHORE

Hamilton

All those years stifled in a small town
It's a shame
I keep thinking I'll see my father
The place looks more or less the same
I can just feel the dysfunction,
       the denial
oozing out of the concrete
I have this feeling of hopelessness
      and doom
           in the pit of my stomach
Racist faces stare out at me
The tone of condescension in their gaze
Why, I feel sick all over again
Gasping for breath
      — fighting to survive

At last
      as I keep moving forward
           there's no looking back

As I speed out of this
      nest of despair
the air becomes clearer
      my body feels lighter
I am leaving it all behind
The church on the way out
      ... a moment of uncertainty ...
Thank you God
I have survived
      I am a survivor
I AM FREE

SHEILA RAMDASS

Illegitimacy

The recording
of my being
was by conspiracy
distorted through inheritance
from parents of Indian ancestry
whose ancient philosophy
by default and ignorance
was depreciated cruelly
by racists and colonial policy

The fallacy
of my illegitimacy
that colonial stigma
of lesser quality
is a betrayed legacy
by a hypocritical nation
sustained by hostility
against Indo-Caribbean people
with indentured history

christened coolie
by French Creole and slavery
a derogatory label
for a stalwart people
whose sweat and deprivation
sustained the same nation,
amidst great confusion
and conspirators' games,
also distorted names

The rewards heaped
as Indians dutifully reaped
and sorrowfully sowed
the Caribbean earth
with sugarcane and sweat
for Europe's benefit
was punctuated with pain,
with endless shame,
and all the fruits of illegitimacy

SYEDA NUZHAT SIDDIQUI

To Human Race

Even though our colours and our names
are not the same
even though our lands
lay asunder
and the space above us
is victim
of plunder
we still are of the one
human clan

Our beginning, the same
our end is the same
our short lives
full of strives
our hopes, our illusions
and our dreams
are the same

The pangs of birth
the giggly laughter of children's mirth
our pleasures, our pains
our dreams are the same
we all belong to the same
domain

All children
of mother Earth
all drenched
in heavenly light
of sound and sight
we share the same seasons
sun, moon, storms
and their flight
we have the same
home and hearth

We are the same
but who did play
this cruel game
of encircling us
with a wall of pain
we are still alive
but who did try
to choke our breath
and to entangle us
in the cobweb of death

Our hearts were clean
and who is the one
who put dust
of mistrust
our minds were

like a star
giving light
near and far
who did play
this cruel game
of turning into smoke
this light and flame

The answer to these questions
is the same
as history of torture
and violence
is the same

Dreams of peace, truth and love
of breaking shackles
spreading our wings
soaring high
in the sky
our dreams are the same

As we are one
we stand
hand in hand
we will then break
the wall of pain
and start again
from the point
where we were
one
belonging to the one human clan

TRANSLATED BY SALEEM SIDDIQUI

CONTRIBUTORS' NOTES

DHARINI ABEYESKERA, born in Sri Lanka, grew up bilingual. Her early ambition was to become an author. At university she pursued linguistics and English as a Second Language with a view to making the "language of power" more accessible. Abeyeskera moved to Toronto in 1990. She is presently a literacy worker in the Junction Triangle area of Toronto where she lives with her partner and son.

FAWZIA AHMAD is a Trinidadian woman proud of her Indian heritage. She works as a rape and crisis worker in British Columbia and is a full-time student. She celebrates brownness. Her fight against racism within the white feminist community tires her out but she will survive as all brown women survive. Thoughts of her family and Trinidad and Tobago are constantly on her mind.

LOPA BANERJEE is a volunteer at Saheli Women's Resource Centre, New Delhi (India), an autonomous women's organization working mainly on the issues of health, violence against women, and laws relating to women. To earn a living she works as a freelance communications consultant. Her abiding interests are writing and acting (both stage and street theatre).

SUDHARSHANA COOMARASAMY has found writing an important outlet from the age of eleven or twelve. During the July 1983 racial riots in Sri Lanka, everything Coomarasamy's family owned was set ablaze, including all her poems. On leaving her country and seeking refuge elsewhere, for the first time she began to write in Tamil, her mother tongue. In 1988, she published a book of Tamil poems in Montreal. She is now working on a collection of English poems.

TSHERING WANGMO DHOMPA is a Tibetan woman currently living in Delhi, India. Dhompa is pursuing her Masters degree in literature. She works as an editor and a freelance journalist, and has been writing poetry for many years. Her work has appeared in *Diva*.

FARZANA DOCTOR was born in Zambia. Her family is from India and she has lived most of her life in Canada. She works as a social worker in Toronto and is a member of the Saheli Theatre Troupe, a feminist, educational, South Asian women's theatre collective.

SHANTI DHORE was conceived in Trinidad and born in Canada. She lives in Toronto and works as an actor for various theatre companies, including Theatre In The Rough. She is currently part of the Saheli Theatre Troupe, a feminist, educational, South Asian women's theatre collective. Dhore has written poetry since she was in her early teens and has works published in *Diva*. She considers her greatest accomplishment that of becoming a single mother.

MARIAM KHAN DURRANI published her first work, *Not To Understand*, a collection of poetry, in 1990, when she was fourteen. She is an anti-racism activist in her high school and has been published by *Diva* and *Fireweed*. Her writing is forthcoming in a youth anthology to be published by Harcourt Brace Canada.

RAMABAI ESPINET was born in Trinidad and Tobago and has lived in Canada for many years. She is a writer of fiction and poetry, a critic and an academic. Her published works include the collection of poetry *Nuclear Seasons* (1991), the anthology *Creation Fire* (1990), which she edited, and the children's books *The Princess of Spadina* (1992) and *Ninja's Carnival* (1993). Her poetry/performance piece, *Indian Robber Talk* (1993), has been recently staged in Toronto.

DAMAYANTHI FERNANDO, is a science teacher by profession. Her first story, "My Sister Alice," won third prize in the Shenlle Creative Writer of the Year 1988, organized in association with The British Council, Sri Lanka. Fernando is also a freelance journalist whose work has been published in periodicals, magazines and newspapers.

NILAMBRI SINGH GHAI performs in plays that reflect the reality of women of South Asian origin in Quebec and Canada. She is a teacher, an employment counselor, a literary tutor, a poet, a mother and an activist. She is on the editorial collective of *Montreal Serai* and a consulting editor of *Diva*, and regularly writes for both. She is a long-time member of Montreal-based South Asian Women's Centre and is currently involved with the Ottawa-based South Asian Women Working Together.

VEENA GOKHALE is a Masters student in Environmental Studies at York University. She has worked as a journalist in Bombay in a former life and now likes to think of herself as an activist with a sense of humour. She is working on a novella titled "Ghost Story." Gokhale came to Canada two years ago and enjoys being Canadian and Indian at one and the same time.

SHERAZAD JAMAL was born in London, England in 1963 and immigrated from Kenya to Canada in 1973. Her education includes a BA in English, a Bachelors in Environmental Design and a Masters in Architecture. Her current primary focus is raising her son, Zakir. Between playtime, diaper changes, naps, meals and cleaning, she designs *Rungh* magazine, manages to produce the occasional piece of art and scribbles notes and observations to herself on odd pieces of paper with the intention of someday having the time and inspiration to write a great novel!

MALIKA JAYASINGHE contributes articles to a national daily newspaper. Her short stories have been published by literary journals in Sri Lanka, where she lives with her four children and partner.

SHEILA JAMES lives and works primarily in Toronto as a theatre artist/activist. Her plays *Canadian Monsoon* (3D Cahoots Festival, Toronto) and *Sex Straight Up Racy Sexy Project* (Vancouver) were staged in 1993. She recently returned from Hyderabad, India, where she performed in various groups and helped establish a feminist theatre group, Chelimi. She continues to have an association with the Company Of Sirens, Cahoots Theatre Projects, Carousel Players, Desh Pardesh, *Diva*, Fresh Arts and *TCAR*. She is a community and social activist.

MAYA KHANKHOJE was born in Mexico to an Indian father and Belgian mother and is the mother of two young women. She started writing in India, stopped for a few years while she raised a family in Mexico, and began writing again in Montreal, where she has been working as a simultaneous interpreter for a United Nations agency for the last sixteen years. She writes mainly in English, although she has published some work in Spanish and French. She has won a few awards for her fiction, poetry and prose. She is involved with the peace movement and women's issues and loves travel, especially on environmental expeditions.

LASANDA KURUKULASURIYA was born in Sri Lanka and immigrated to Canada a few years ago. Her articles have appeared in *Herizons*, *The New Internationalist*, *Now*, *Diva*, *Sawasdee* and *Intermedia*. In Sri Lanka she wrote for several newspapers and magazines and coedited *The Shenelle Book of Sri Lankan Short Stories* (1988).

MINA KUMAR was born in Madras, India, and lived in Singapore, Toronto and Los Angeles before coming to New York City. Her fiction has appeared in *Christopher Street*, *Turnstile*, *Diva* and *Short Fiction by Women*. Her poetry has appeared in *Fireweed*, *Manushi*, *Long Shot*, *Room of One's Own*, *The Toronto Review of Contemporary Writing Abroad* and *Premonitions* (Kaya). She has also written for several magazines including *Ms*, *Belles Letters*, *Deneuve*, *Rungh*, *Sojourner* and *India Currents*.

KISHWAR NAHEED is perhaps the most prolific Urdu poet of her generation in Pakistan. Her poems range from traditional love lyrics to political pieces addressing a variety of feminist issues. Naheed edited the prestigious monthly, *Maah-i-Nau*, for several years and has translated poetry into Urdu. She has published several volumes of poetry, including *Lips that Speak*, *Unnamed Journey*, *Poems*, *Alleyways: the Sun: Doorways*, *Amidst Approaches* and *The Colour Pink*. Two of her collections of poetry have been translated into English.

UMA PARAMESWARAN was born in Madras and raised in Nagpur and Jabalpur, in India. She was the recipient of a Smith-Mundt Fulbright fellowship to study English literature in the United States, where she received her Doctorate from Michigan State University in 1972. She came to Canada in 1966, and currently teaches Post-Colonial Literature at the University of Winnipeg. She was the founder of Pali (Performing Arts & Literature of India) to organize formal dance instruction and is a producer of a weekly television show. Her poems have appeared in *Nimrod, Canadian Literature, CV2* and in several Indian periodicals. She is the author of three volumes of fiction, poetry and drama including *Trishanku* (1988).

ANOLI PERERA's art has been deeply influenced by the cultural traditions of Sri Lanka, which span over two thousand years. A self-taught artist and a keen observer of detail, she uses as her media pastels, pencil, oils, watercolours and acrylic. Though the dominant themes in her work continue to be influenced by memories and experiences from Sri Lanka, Perera has recently expanded her range to include cultural experiences from such diverse places as South America and Africa.

FAUZIA RAFIQ is a peace-loving woman continually being made to fight in order to live in peace. Ambitious, she aspires to write poetry, sing, paint, make her own pottery, live among wild flowers and beside a clear-water lake. In reality, however, she is a fiction writer and a resource-developer, cannot sing at all, paints only T-shirts, buys her pottery from various garage sales each summer, picks up hydroponically grown flowers from convenience stores across the street, works for neglible amounts of money for *Diva* and *Dark*, and lives right beside a TTC bus stop. Still, she believes her contribution to be of much value.

SHEILA RAMDASS was born in Trinidad of East Indian ancestry. She is now a Canadian citizen and lives in Scarborough, Ontario. Her writings reflect her concerns about universal human deprivation and discrimination, particularly the suppression and struggles of women. Some of her writings also provide insight into her Indo-Caribbean heritage and her experiences growing up in a colonial society. She is currently working on an anthology of short stories and a collection of poetry.

ARCHANA SHARMA was born in Punjab, India in 1970 and immigrated to Toronto with her family in 1973. She is a recent graduate from the University of Toronto and struggles to live, write and love in the city.

SYEDA NUZHAT SIDDIQUI, poet, writer and educator, is the cofounder of World University of Peace in Toronto. She is the author of *Nida-i-Amn* [Voice of Peace], and received the Aalami

Urdu Award from the international Urdu Conference held in Delhi, India in 1987. Born in Pakistan, she now lives in Toronto.

RINA SINGH was born in India and came to Canada in 1980. She is the author of *Selected Poems* (Writer's Workshop, Calcutta). Her poems and stories have appeared in Canadian literary journals. She has a Masters in Creative Writing from Concordia University, Montreal. After securing a teaching degree from McGill University in Montreal, she taught creative writing there for many years. Also an artist, she has exhibited oil paintings in Montreal. She is presently teaching in Toronto, where she now lives.

RENUKA SOOKNANAN was born in Port of Spain, Trinidad of working-class parents. She immigrated to Canada in 1974 at the age of six, a year after her parents' settlement. She is presently a Doctoral candidate at York University. Her academic writing is focussed on theorizing immigrants women's volunteer community work. She began writing poetry at the age of twelve. For Sooknanan, poetry is a political process of questioning; it is a collective art inscribing people, history, voice and, in the end, solidarity.

VINITA SRIVASTAVA lives in Toronto. She works as a radio artist, poet, writer and social activist.

SHAHNAZ STRI was born in Bombay and came to Canada in 1976. She has written poetry from the age of ten. She was a contributor to *A Piece Of My Heart* (Sister Vision Press) and is working on a collection of poetry and prose.

ZARA SULEMAN is an East African, South Asian, Muslim cultural activist, artist, writer, feminist of Colour, rape crisis worker and full-time Communications and Women's Studies student at Simon Fraser University in British Columbia. Suleman has also worked in theatre arts and film in directing, script writing, lighting and acting. The issues of race, representation, and South Asian women and sexuality are her main research concerns.

SUNERA THOBANI was born in Bukoba, Tanzania. She came to Canada in 1989. Thobani helped organize against the opening of sex selection clinics in British Columbia and was a founding member of SAWAN (South Asian Women's Network). She was elected

President of the National Action Committee on the Status of Women (NAC), the largest feminist organization in Canada, in 1993. She is a single mother.

SMITA VIR TYAGI is a psychologist by training. Many of her poems are rooted in her experiences as a therapist. She has lived and worked in India for several years and has written extensively on women's issues, psychiatry and mental health. She has only recently dared venture into creative writing. She now lives in Toronto and works with a family services agency counselling victims of physical and sexual violence.

GLOSSARY

abbu – (Urdu) father

amma – (Urdu/Hindi) mother

anna – (Hindi) former monetary unit of Burma, India and Pakistan equal to one-sixteenth of a rupee

Aurat Durbar – (Hindi/Urdu) The court of women. Term of empowerment created by Rita Kohli in 1989 for *Diva*. It redefines the words *aurat* (commonly used to denote a state of powerlessness) and *durbar* (commonly used for the court of a male monarchy) to reflect the self-empowerment of women.

avacka – gourd-like vegetable

avial – mixed vegetable sauce

ayah – (Urdu/Hindi) nanny

badami – (Urdu) from *badam*, almond; denotes shade of brown; used to complement skin colour

balem – (Urdu/Hindi) lover

behenjee – (Urdu) older sister

bhaji – curry

bhang – (Urdu/Hindi) hemp (cannabis) leaves and tips ground, boiled in water and mixed with almond, cardamom and sugar

bindi – the red dot on the forehead traditionally worn by married Hindu women

burka – (Urdu) veil worn by some Muslim women as a sign of modesty

calaloo – West Indian dish specific to Trinidad

chai – (Urdu/Hindi) tea

chandahar – (Urdu/Hindi) a type of necklace

charpayee – (Urdu) a bed consisting of a frame strung with rope

chena – chick peas

churidar – close-fitting pyjama worn with *kurta*

covacka – gourd

dal – cooking grain; e.g. lentils

dal-chawal – *dal* and rice

dopatta – (Urdu) head veil or kerchief worn by Muslim women as a sign of modesty

dudhwala – (Urdu/Hindi) milkman

galli – narrow alley

ghazal – (Persian/Arabic/Urdu) a verse form with a set rhyme scheme and stanza pattern

goche – tomato sauce

jee – yes; also term of respect used following title

Kama Sutra – pre-Vedic text on love and sex

keema-mutter – minced meat and peas

khaddar – (Hindi) handspun cotton cloth

kurta – dress worn on top of *shalwar*

laddu – type of sweet

maulvi – (Urdu) Muslim priest

meena bai – house servant

mela – fair

memsahib – title for European woman

miya – husband

naan – type of flatbread; roti

orhni – (Hindi) *dopatta*; cloth used to cover a woman's head and upper body

pallu – corner of *dopatta*, sari

patani kute – (Tamil) pea-based sauce

pauwalla – breadman

pavacka – gourd

paysam – type of dessert

pdalanga sambar – (Hindi) lentil-based sauce

porichche kute – (Tamil) sauce

pushnika morqoyambe – pumpkin sauce

raam naam satya hai – (Hindi) the name of God is the truth

rasam – (Tamil) sauce

sambar – (Tamil) lentil sauce

shalwar, shalwar kameez – Punjabi suit for women; the *dopatta* is part of the suit

suttee – (Sanskrit) the custom requiring Hindu widows to cremate themselves on their husband's funeral pyre as an indication of devotion

thali – plate for food

PUBLICATION DATA

Materials listed below as first published in *Diva: Art and Literary Journal of Women of South Asian Origin* are reprinted courtesy *Diva* and the authors.

Abeyeskera, Dharini. "From the Don Valley Parkway" and "Tactics." *Diva*, 4: 2.

Espinet, Ramabai. "Dare to Bare." *Diva*, 3: 4 (January, 1993.)

Gokhale, Veena. "Reveries Of A Riot." *Diva*, 4:1 (June, 1993).

James, Sheila. "Indian Woman/English Man." *Resources for Feminist Research (RFR/DRF)*, 21: 3/4. "From Promiscuity to Celibacy: A Creative Piece on Sexuality." *Diva*, 3: 4 (January, 1993).

Khankhoje, Maya. "The Transistor Radio." Published in French in *Montreal Serai*. Published in English in *Los*, Concordia University, (1981). "The Watershed." Winner in a contest organized by a local newspaper and a conference on ageing.

Kumar, Mina. "There is No Place Like Home." *13th Moon*.

Naheed, Kishwar. Poems translated from the Urdu. In *The Scream of an Illegitimate Voice*. Lahore, Pakistan: Sang-e-Meel Publications, 1991.